JIMBO

A Novel of Resurgence and Redemption

JOE CAWLEY

iUniverse, Inc.
New York Bloomington

JIMBO
A Novel of Resurgence and Redemption

iUniverse books may be ordered through booksellers or by contacting:

iUniverse
1663 Liberty Drive
Bloomington, IN 47403
www.iuniverse.com
1-800-Authors (1-800-288-4677)

ISBN: 978-1-4502-3757-4 (pbk)
ISBN: 978-1-4502-3759-8 (cloth)
ISBN: 978-1-4502-3758-1 (ebook)

Printed in the United States of America

iUniverse rev. date: 7/8/10

To JIMBO

A Backward Glance

It is well when you've lived in clover
To mourn for the days gone by –
Would I live the same life over
Could I live again? Not I!
But, knowing the false from the real
I would strive to ascend
I would seek out my boyhood's ideal
And follow it to the end.

Henry Lawson

Acknowledgments

I would like to thank the following people:

My wife, Margie O'Malley Cawley provided me with guidance throughout the time it has taken to finish writing this novel. Her patience and understanding were invaluable.

Lynn Cawley Israel and Christie Cawley Knott provided editorial input which helped shape the unruly manuscript into a final draft.

Many others provided support. Some doing so without ever knowing.

Chapter 1

His brother, Jim, had promised to be there. Not quite in blood but close to it in Joe's mind. The promise had taken place at their last meeting, which had shockingly occurred in New York City on September 8, 2001, in the lobby of the World Trade Center.

Their totally unexpected, life-altering meeting had been their first sight of each other in over three decades. Brother Jim had died in Vietnam back in '68, or so the family back home had believed for thirty-three years. Then he re-entered Joe's life like a heaven-sent bolt of lightning to a rusted lightning rod and was just as quickly gone, once more out of sight before the thunder had time to announce his presence.

Jim McDonnell was intentionally the last invitee to arrive at the reception that Saturday evening, September 8, 2001. He went unnoticed among the throng of 150 good-hearted New Yorkers that had gathered there by invitation for a charitable event. The book signing in the lobby of the World Trade Center was the last part of an all-evening progressive fund-raiser for a national charity.

Jim bided his time until he was positioned as the last of the guests to line up to have a book signed. He then casually presented Joe McDonnell with a copy of Joe's novel, *Hallowed Gesture*. Jim had already addressed the inside of the cover: *To Jimbo from big brother Joe. Long time no see. With brotherly love …*

An exhausted Joe McDonnell reached for the book as it was directed toward him. He momentarily smiled and glanced about the immediate area. His mood was lighthearted and jovial; the crowd and the questions had been friendly and noninvasive all evening. With the last signing, the gala event would soon draw to a close, and he would have delivered on his reluctant promise to participate. Though this was his first book signing, the reclusive writer was damn sure it would also be his last.

Refocusing on the task before him, he looked down at the open book in his tired hands. This would be the final signature of the evening. One hundred and fifty patrons had won an entry ticket in an Internet raffle, and every one of them had attended.

Joe casually read the scripted greeting and thought it was most unusual. After reading it silently, he mouthed *Jimbo* repeatedly to himself. He then slowly and deliberately moved his eyes upward as he felt the rush of mixed emotion. At first he felt pissed off, as if someone was messing with his mind. His angry gaze darted upward and became transfixed as he met his brother's eyes for the first time in over thirty years. Jimbo had been Jim's boyhood nickname, surviving only in Joe's mind until that face-to-face moment in slow-motion time. The man's smiled response through a whiskered face told Joe that, indeed, it was his brother, back from the "missing and presumed dead."

Jim, without saying a word, motioned with a double sideward flick of his head, and Joe blindly followed Jim's unspoken request to follow him outside. The two abruptly left their respective sitting and standing positions and took a single file walk toward the entrance door.

The meeting, though intentionally executed by Brother Jim, was brief and off guard. It left Joe in unaccustomed silent compliance. Jim hurriedly and hastily briefed him on Blue Seas Enterprises (BSE), the international covert company of which he was a founding principal. He warned of impending terror and said Joe needed to flee New York City that very night.

This mysterious, almost mystical visit carried a possible life-saving message for not only Joe to immediately leave NYC but also for his wife, Maggie, to immediately leave Washington, D.C., where she was visiting their friend Julia. Jim gave few details other than, "Tell no one. Do not fly. Travel by car. Leave for Florida this evening, and make sure Maggie takes Julia with her."

With his intended warning message delivered directly on target, Jim turned to leave. Almost as an afterthought, he turned on a dime back toward Joe and added, with a slight half smile on his face, "I'll see you over the holidays at your home in Florida. In fact, I'll see you at Thanksgiving."

Joe's response was an astonished stone-faced, silent up-and-down nod.

Jim then slipped past the open rear door and into the backseat of a waiting Mercedes limousine. He sent a quick glance back at Joe as he pulled the door closed behind him. The black car promptly drove off and faded into the darkness of the night.

Joe stood motionlessly as he visually followed the red taillights of the conveyance until it was out of sight. Then, after gathering himself, he put Jim's directive into motion. First, he went directly to his hotel, made some quick notes, packed his bag, and checked out. Next, he made a quick successful call to Maggie at Julia's place and delivered Jim's dire warning. Then he arranged a quick limo ride and headed directly out of town. He was gone from NYC within an hour, and while en route, he tried to reach his agent, Jerry Sewickley, by cell phone without success.

His first stop was at a car rental facility near Allentown, Pennsylvania. By then it was early morning, just before dawn, and Joe and his driver parted company. While the limo headed back to NYC, Joe proceeded toward Harrisburg, Pennsylvania, in a gray Buick from National Car Rental. Just east of Harrisburg, he merged onto I-81 south and mentally planned to cut back east to I-95 somewhere south of D.C.

The drive down I-81 in the dawning hours of Sunday morning brought his adrenaline high down to a manageable level. With the whine of the tires now-white noise, the miles began to pass by quietly in the night as his mind regained reasonable function.

Joe began to process what had happened between the book signing and the disappearing taillights of the Mercedes that had carried his brother out of sight. He had always had good recall for details, and he was sure his mental review had missed nothing. He went back over the evening again and again in his mind. Something kept bugging him about their brief meeting, but try as he might, he was unable to conjure up a clue.

Now well south of Washington, D.C., he welcomed the sight of the morning light. He tried to make a decision whether he should stop for some sleep or continue to push on toward Florida. And that was when the realization hit him square in the face. That moment drove all tiredness out of his mind.

The moment he had looked up at the face of the man who had placed the open book in front of him to sign, Joe had immediately known that the face, though covered in a neatly trimmed beard, was the face of his brother. His conviction had grown as he had looked into the eyes of the man; it had indeed been his brother. In addition, as they had stood outside on the sidewalk while Joe listened and Jim spoke, Joe had known beyond any reasonable doubt that the fellow was his long-lost and presumed-dead sibling.

However, it was what Joe had not seen that ate a hole in him hours later. Brother Jim had not displayed either in his mannerisms or in his body language any indication that he recognized Joe as his brother. All of his actions had sought recognition from Joe, but he had given nothing in return; it had been as though he was talking to a complete stranger. Joe was unable to reconcile this nagging dilemma as he drove, and he slowly exhausted his thoughts on the subject. He resolved to just focus on the drive.

A long twenty-four hours later, now Sunday night, he arrived safely home and impatiently waited for Maggie and Julia to arrive. He was ahead of them by twelve hours because they had stopped overnight while en route. He was damn near exhausted with relief when they arrived safely on late Monday morning.

Maggie and Joe had planned to visit Julia at her apartment in Washington, D.C., that weekend. However, when Joe had received a request to help his publisher with a charitable event in NYC, he had been unable to refuse. Joe had not been the first choice for the book signing event. He had been more of a last-minute replacement. Nevertheless, he had agreed to help out, and due to the curious nature of his novel, there had been a very acceptable level of interest when they added him to the evening's agenda.

Julia Bond had met Joe in Scranton, Pennsylvania, shortly after he had arrived to make arrangements to reinter his brother's remains to Arlington National Cemetery. She had been in Scranton on an undercover assignment with the FBI. They had met solely by chance, and Joe had actually found himself on the fringe of her FBI investigation due to his relationship with some of the characters Julia and her partner, Ferp Webster, had under surveillance.

Julia and Joe had developed a relationship that had almost led them down an emotionally careless road; however, by the end of the FBI investigation, Julia and Joe had resolved their situation by deciding that being good friends was exactly the right relationship for them. Eventually, Maggie and Joe had become parental figures to Julia, filling a void in her emotional life left by the untimely deaths of both of her parents when she was a child.

Julia had left the FBI and eventually joined the same intelligence firm Mike McDonnell, Joe's son, worked for. Mike had made contact with Julia during the course of his intelligence activities and had convinced Julia to become a part of the Blue Seas Organization. At the time, Mike and Julia discovered that they had a common acquaintance—a character by the name of Joe McDonnell.

It was close to noon on Monday when Maggie and Julia pulled into the McDonnell driveway. They spotted Joe's rental car and both heaved a sigh of relief. Leaving their car in the driveway, they scrambled through the front door of the McDonnell household. Joe met them in the foyer. The women dropped their bags and followed as he hastily led them farther into the comfort of the spacious house.

They gathered in the kitchen, and Joe relayed to them what had occurred in NYC. As outlandish as it sounded, his scenario provided them with a sense of relief on one hand and a sense of foreboding on the other. Their relief came from the fact that they could see him face-to-face, and physically and mentally, he looked sound. When he had called them in D.C. with an abbreviated, almost cryptic warning—"Get out of town tonight. Drive directly south to home. No airplanes. I'll meet you there. Speak to no one. Danger is everywhere. Make sure Julia leaves with you. Don't take no for an answer"—they both had thought he had finally gone over the edge.

Maggie and Julia had listened intently, unconsciously and simultaneously deciding not to interrupt him until he finished. They were spellbound by the smooth, deliberate unfolding of Joe's story, and they were compelled to believe every word of it. From the onset, the appearance of his brother out of nowhere after thirty years was intriguing. But at the same time, they were worried that the tale could not possibly be the product of a rational mind.

Joe finished his play-by-play relay of events and finally stopped talking. The women's first knowing glance at each other betrayed their fear, but Joe beat them to the draw.

"I know you both think I am crazy."

"No, Joe—" Maggie started to speak, but he interrupted her.

"Listen carefully to what I am about to tell you." As he continued to speak, he alternately looked them both directly in the eye. "If someone had just told me this story under these same circumstances, I would think he should be immediately committed to a mental institution."

Once again, Maggie and Julia's head-nodding immediately identified their mindsets and betrayed their silent thoughts. They were not buying what he was selling, but they were willing to continue listening to him because they were unable to verbalize their thoughts.

Again, Joe spoke up. "Let me give you something that will help you understand and, more importantly, believe me." Before he continued, he slowly rose from his seat.

Julia quickly asked, "Where are you going? Are you getting a drink? If so, I think we all could use one or more."

Another negative head twist from Maggie went ignored. Joe returned to the table with a well-aged bottle of red wine and a familiar corkscrew. He handed both to Maggie. She dismissively passed them to Julia while keeping her eyes on Joe. He once more turned and walked away from them.

Maggie damn well did not want him to start drinking at this hour of the day, at least not before having some lunch. Her mental litany only added to her anguish as Joe then returned with three tall wine glasses, which he gently placed on the table in front of her. He remained standing and then abruptly turned away once again. "I'll be right back," he said softly over his shoulder.

Maggie continued drilling the back of his head with her eyes until he left the kitchen. Then, turning to Julia, she shook her head left to right in wide-eyed disbelief at what had just unfolded in front of them.

While Julia hastily twisted the corkscrew, Maggie began, "Julia, what the—"

Maggie came up short as Joe re-entered the kitchen and once more took his place at the table. He had been out of sight only moments as he cut through the dining room to reach the front foyer, where his briefcase had been haphazardly dashed against his suitcase. Upon returning to the table, he opened the retrieved case just as the cork announced its freedom from the bottle. Julia poured, and Maggie passed the first glass to Joe and took the second for herself. Julia poured a glass for herself and placed the cork back into the half-full bottle. The ball was back in Joe's court.

Long sips were had by all, without comment, as Joe made his next move. Deftly, he removed a white plastic hotel laundry bag from his briefcase and placed it directly in front of them. He then gently opened it and exposed its contents for the two skeptical ladies to review.

It was a copy of Joe's novel, *Hallowed Gesture*, but not just any copy. It was the copy his brother, Jim, had handed to him for his autograph just the night before. It was the same copy that contained the handwritten note and the same copy he hoped would prove to them that he was still in control of his facilities.

They looked, and they read. They nodded. He had made his point.

Julia spoke as Maggie moved from her seat to give Joe a hug, "Do you suppose he left his fingerprints on this copy?"

"I'm counting on that Julia." Joe smiled as he finished, for he had anticipated her question. His next sip of red wine quickly followed.

Joe knew that Julia, in her prior position with the FBI, could not only run the prints but could also access Jim's military file and compare them. He also knew that despite the overwhelming demands being placed on the FBI, she could do it practically overnight should she so desire. About that he had no doubt.

It was a long wait that evening and into the morning. They sat up late into the night. Joe drank red wine, Julia sipped it, and Maggie quit early and fell asleep on the couch. If the prints and military record matched up, it would confirm beyond any doubt that Brother Jim was alive and well. Joe had no doubt; his anxiety over gaining resolution was fueled by Maggie's and Julia's lingering doubts. He knew they were both wrestling hard with their doubts and their fears about his own mental well-being.

The next day, early in the morning of September 11, the FBI report was faxed to the house, and Julia gathered Maggie and Joe to review it. Once again, Julia had called in some favors a few people in the bureau owed her, and the results boded well. Everything had checked out. The prints were indeed those of Jim McDonnell, the long-departed marine, and the handwriting analysis—based on Jim's old military file—was close enough. Joe was off the hook with his girls.

They gathered around the kitchen table. Joe had been first to the kitchen that morning, and he cooked breakfast. The ladies verbalized their guilt about doubting him as they finished breakfast and moved to the comfort of the cozy den. However, their guilt had long passed by the end of their second cups of coffee. The horror of 9/11 blasted into the world and across the airways. In the McDonnell household, the subject abruptly changed to Jimbo.

"How could he have known?" They were totally perplexed.

They spent the following days in quiet anguish as they absorbed the impact of the horror perpetuated by the terrorist attack. Like many other good people of the world, they looked on in disbelief as the clips of the initial impacts of the airliners' deliberate flights into the twin towers were played over and over on all the networks. The clips were immediately followed by video of the total implosion of the buildings. The billowing plumes of grey smoke and dust choked the air as rescuers rushed forward in response only to lose their lives. All thoughts on any other subjects were put on indefinite hold.

Weeks later, the shock of 9/11 still reverberated around the world as time quickly moved into mid-October. Maggie and Joe continuously watched the news in silent disbelief as they shared the absolute terror of what their country and fellow citizens were absorbing. Their own inside information of their preemptive personal awareness still shocked them into silence. They could not talk about it. Jim had warned of the danger, and they had not known the extent of what he meant. They would silently wait to see him at Thanksgiving.

An unwelcome, unrelenting Nor'easter extended into its third day, continuing to drench northern Florida. The heavy, grey, overcast skies only added to the gloom of the aftermath of 9/11. The leaves were turning colors farther north, and the heartbreaking search and cleanup continued in Manhattan. It was a really a very bad time in America. Joe sat at his desk and stared out at the windblown Atlantic while pondering the thoughts racing around in his mind.

Damn it! He had been expecting a call from Jim, and with each passing day and any and every mention of Thanksgiving, Joe's fuse burned shorter and shorter. He mentally attempted to *will* the goddamn promised call into being. He began to pace …

Chapter 2

Joe McDonnell and Maggie had been happily married for thirty-four years. They had gone through some tough times in the '90s. Joe had been knocked on his ass by a mental illness doctors had medically confirmed as depression. His depression had cost him his livelihood and nearly cost him his sanity. Against all odds, he had come out the other end of the tunnel without being run over by the proverbial train. It took every ounce of love and caring for them to survive the illness individually and for their marriage to survive as well.

Fortunately, Joe had been loaded with stock options from his previous employment and proceeded to cash out at a most opportune time. In the fall of 1998, Joe and Maggie had made plans to relocate from New York State to Florida to begin a new life together. When Maggie had left for Florida to oversee the design and construction of their new house, Joe had gone off on a tangent to settle a long-lingering, gut-wrenching desire to honor his deceased brother's childhood wish to be buried in Arlington National Cemetery. Maggie encouraged him, thinking it was a deep-rooted mental issue that had caused a lot of Joe's mental unrest. In reality, she was very far from the root of Joe's illness. Joe had carried a secret burden back from Vietnam that he and he alone would bear.

His brother, Jim, had died in Vietnam. He had been a Huey pilot, and as the story went, he had been shot out of the night sky near the Vietnam/Laotian border while on a mission. A long, heart-aching delay that was never explained ensued before his remains finally completed the long, silent plane ride to Dover AFB in Dover, Delaware. The body, zipped up in black plastic and secured inside a nondescript government-issued brushed aluminum casket had been off-loaded to an awaiting hearse and quietly driven home to the valley of his birth. Jim's stamp of arrival had read, *Sealed. Not for viewing.*

Joe had been a reluctant combat marine grunt serving in Vietnam at the same time his brother landed in-country. Joe's mail piled up back at his home base, and thus neither of them had been aware that the other was in Vietnam. Joe had been in combat for four months and, like the others around him, had been convinced he would never leave there alive. His last action was to honor the code and shoot several severely wounded fellow marines who requested—no, demanded with their last labored breath—that he "do it."

When he had been hastily summoned by his superiors to report to Danang, he had figured he was a goner. Someone must of gotten wind his act of regret, but to his ultimate surprise, he had been informed he was about to be reborn as a civilian. The good news was coupled with the matter-of-fact statement that his brother had been killed in action the evening before.

Thanks to the political machinations of his family's congressman, who happened to chair the Armed Services Committee, Joe had been summarily discharged. He went home and never spoke of the war again until some thirty years later when he announced he was honoring his deceased brother's wish.

While Joe was off in their old hometown arranging the reinternment of his brother's body, he met Julia Bond under the most unusual circumstances. Julia, an FBI agent, and her male partner were on a special assignment in Scranton, Pennsylvania. The nature of their undercover operation had overlapped with occurrences involving some of Joe's old hometown, life-long friends and Joe's mission to move his brother's body to Arlington. The overlap had proved to be nothing more than coincidence.

However, Joe had never finished the rather extraordinary but seemingly uncomplicated process of moving his brother's remains to Arlington. Devastated, he had decided to remain behind in his old hometown and live in the family apartment. He had inherited the eleven-unit apartment building from his mother's very modest estate ten years earlier. There, he had spent his time drinking excessively and attempting to write a fictional novel about the strange occurrences that had unfolded all around him since his arrival back in Scranton. Joe had been trying to reach closure over the bizarre events that had wrapped him in a jacket of controversy since his arrival back in the valley of his birth.

Things had just gone horribly wrong for him. He was physically and mentally wasted. Eventually, in the early fall of 2000 and with much dismay, he had moved to Florida to be with Maggie in their new home. However, he *did* succeed in getting his novel published, and this accomplishment seemed to get him back on a straight, though rocky, road.

Joe McDonnell was an old-school guy in his fifties. He was five foot ten, 185 pounds, and topped off with a head of silver hair. He now kept himself in good physical shape and had become extremely proficient in martial arts. Mentally, he wrestled on and off with bouts of depression. In fact, he had traveled some hard miles in his life, and many of those roads had been unpaved. He was still married after thirty-four years to his younger wife, Maggie. He listed his occupation as fiction writer. His first, and to date his only, novel had been published well over a year before in 2000. Unexpectedly, and to his eternal gratitude, the novel had been quite well received. At the very end of this freshman novel, he promised—as Paul Harvey would say—"the rest of the story."

He was now wrestling with the self-imposed pressure from being overdue to deliver a second novel. Concurrently, the members of his literary inner circle—comprised of his wife Maggie; his old friend and extremely supportive literary agent, Paul Burke; and his publisher, Jerry Sewickley— all concurred.

Joe's mind had been elsewhere lately. He was easily agitated and full of anticipation. Maggie attributed his recent behavior to his normally manageable attention deficit disorder, and she encouraged him to stay on track with his writing. She knew once he got into a story, his compulsive nature would take over and drive him forward as though he were on literary autopilot.

However, he was just unable to get any legs under the project. The nonevent hurricane season was waning, and the gorgeous fall weather would soon be upon them, bringing forth all the outdoor activities they loved, especially the long, cozy walks on the beach. The Thanksgiving holiday was also just over the horizon. Joe had been silently counting down to this particular holiday since September.

As a result of their meeting in Scranton, Julia and Joe had become close friends—almost too close. Later, with more grounded emotions, Maggie and Joe had literally become mother and father figures to Julia, and they visited each other quite often. Julia, who was in her thirties, was a knockout. The stars in Hollywood had nothing on her, and she had been a top-notch FBI agent to boot. Internally, she had been quietly admired by her coworkers and superiors for her intelligence and innate abilities. The only negative back-room verbalization from her superiors was, "Too bad she's a female."

Maggie and Joe had one child. Their son Mike was a Villanova University graduate and an officer in the Marine Corps. He and Joe were distant due to Mike's choice of occupation. Joe became pissed off the day Mike informed him of his decision to join the Corps upon graduation, and he stayed pissed until several months ago when Julia interceded on Mike's behalf, though unknown to Mike, and badgered Joe into submission. Maggie had thoroughly enjoyed the process, for she had given up on her son and husband ever reconciling.

Mike never spoke of his actual military occupation other than to say every marine was a rifleman first. He was deeply involved with intelligence gathering and oftentimes went about plying his trade in civilian clothing that matched the attire common to the particular location of interest. Unbeknownst to all, Mike had resigned from the Corp and joined Blue Seas Enterprises in late summer of '01.

Maggie, Julia, and Mike gathered at the McDonnell's House, the week prior to the holiday, all anticipating the promised pre Thanksgiving Day phone call and subsequent arrival of Jim McDonnell. At this juncture, they only knew—as relayed to them by "big brother" Joe—that Jimbo was a former marine helicopter pilot in Vietnam, and he had been shot down and presumed killed. Jim's sudden resurgence had electrified them all.

Chapter 3

The date was April 25, 1968. It was the last mission of the day. Jimbo's Huey was light; its fuel was low, and the ammo was about spent. The rocket pods were empty, and the door machine gunners' 60s had been quiet since they left the battle site.

The sun melted brilliantly into the horizon at its usual speed of 1,000 miles per hour. In the distance, the Huey known by the call sign Tundra 6 headed for home base at its top speed of 125 miles per hour. Darkness would soon move in at a quickening pace, and everyone on board the helicopter wanted to be on the ground before darkness engulfed them.

The crew was as familiar with the routine as they were with each other, with one exception. As of last week, they had a new captain. The green, young lieutenant copilot in the left front seat was familiar to the rest of the crew, and two enlisted men—both about seven months into their mandatory thirteen-month tours of duty—manning the back-to-back M60 door guns were long-time members. Overseeing the function and safety of the craft and crew was the sergeant. He was the NCO, (non-commissioned officer) and functioned as the crew chief. This was his second tour of duty. He loved the work. The new captain was commanding the flight and crew from the right front seat of the bird. His handle was Jimbo.

The haggard crew had lost their last skipper only a week before as they were returning to base with him still strapped into the right front seat of the Huey. While looking to his right to survey the damage he and his crew had leveled on the faceless enemies below, he had taken a single shot to the face and died instantly.

Summarily, the new captain had lost his entire crew on the same mission. They had been making a low pass to commence raking the enemy position with deadly accurate rocket and machine gun fire. The crew, with typical marine accuracy, had inflicted extremely heavy damage to the unfortunate bastards below. As the Huey had maneuvered in an abrupt upward climb out of harm's way, the roll of the aggressor was unintentionally reversed. The pursuer had become the pursued, and some of the resulting rounds of returned enemy ground fire had disabled the craft and forced it to abruptly crash-land right in the middle of the fierce but scattered fighting below.

The crew had survived the crash and individually, in a defensive half-bent-over running position, moved rapidly and omni directional as they sought refuge from the smoking hulk of their Huey and the intense enemy ground fire that came at them from untold directions.

Two of their fellow gunships had immediately provided withering cover fire long enough for Captain Jim McDonnell to drag one of his wounded crew into the cover of the bush. It had been every man for himself as they found themselves literally dumped into a killing field that was partially of their own making.

Jim had instinctively maneuvered in a zigzag foot pattern to avoid capture by the enemy or their deadly AK-47 rifle fire. He had reached momentary safety by melding into the surrounding bush while shielding his wounded crew member. He had then carried the wounded man farther from the fighting and secured himself and his wounded crewman in the thick deep foliage of the surrounding bush. Only a gulp of air and a silent prayer had separated them from the marauding enemy.

The intensity of the heavy ground fighting had begun to fade after an agonizing fifteen minutes, followed immediately by sporadic fire. The enemy had withdrawn; they knew from experience the exact routine that would follow.

Reinforcements had begun to arrive by air, and they would mop up the area for however long it took. The enemy survivors that could faded into the bush, and the wounded they had left behind were dispatched by the newly arriving troops. There had been no prisoners that day.

A familiar lull, welcomed by most, had fallen over the battle area. This nondescript, piece-of-shit real estate that a rational person wouldn't give a plug nickel for had been baptized in blood. Someone in the rear, someone who would never set eyes on the site, would soon assign a name to it and note its location on a map for posterity.

During the course of the cleanup, as if on cue, the Medevac choppers had arrived to ferry out the wounded and dead marines. There were plenty of both. An exhausted Captain Jim McDonnell had staggered into that scene. Unknown to him, he had been carrying the sole surviving member of his crew on his back. The war was over for that shot-up Marine; the severity of his wounds would be his sorry ticket home.

The rest of the fallen chopper crew had been lifted out of the area in body bags. Captain Jim McDonnell had soon lost the nickname of Jimbo and had been newly christened by his squadron, though much against his wish, as Jungle Jim. He had been immediately assigned to another Huey—Tundra 6. The Jungle Jim handle hadn't survived long before it was replaced by Jim's original handle of Jimbo.

Every Tundra 6 crewmember was tight-lipped as their new captain relayed the message he had just received: "Detour men. We're not going to nest just yet."

They were directed to make a quick diversion from their assigned route to their home base in order to meet up with a marine recognizance patrol that had reported capturing a high-value prisoner somewhere along the Ho Chi Minh trail.

A landing zone had been selected by the recon patrol, and the coordinates were eventually relayed to the crew of Tundra 6. The simple plan was that the ground marines would drop smoke upon the arrival of the Huey. It was easy to plan, quick off the lips, and goddamn deadly to do. They all knew it; those on the ground knew it, and those in the air sure as hell knew it. Green smoke would mean the zone was not hot. Red … well, they would just hope for green.

Talk about being in the wrong place at the wrong time. Tundra 6 stayed over its last target as the other Huey gunships headed for home base. They all agreed that it didn't make a hell of a lot of sense to carry excess ammo home with them, so the captain decided to make one more pass at the enemy. They actually made several more passes over the enemy position, hoping to bring some needed firepower to bear on them. They knew the guys on the ground always appreciated air support.

It was quiet for a spell, and then the few hopeful questions and answers were delivered in rapid fire in a matter of fact way:

"Captain, do we have enough fuel to make the pickup and still reach home base?"

"Affirmative, damn it." The captain's wry response did not go unnoticed by the crew, and he quickly followed with a question of his own. "Enough ammo to fight our way in and out, sarge?"

"Negative, Captain."

"Figures, Sergeant," the captain responded casually as his voice trailed off. He had already known the damn answer. *Wrong place, wrong time*, he thought as he looked at the fading light of day through the scratched and dirty Plexiglas screen that separated his line of vision from the hostile world below them.

Goddamn recon, he thought to himself. Drop them in the middle of the enemy territory, wait a day or two, and then come running like hell to pick them up in a hot spot full of enemy fire. It just didn't make a hell of a lot of sense to him. Now, going in hell-bent for leather, firing rockets and machine guns on known enemy positions day or night—that made sense to him.

Recon always seemed to come back with no prisoners, carrying their dead and wounded, and feeling good about whatever it was that they had just accomplished as their mission. He just didn't get it. Recon guys were just too good to be going out this way, but that seemed to be the rule rather than the exception in this war.

These recon guys are tough sons-of-bitches, he thought.

He had admired them mostly from a distance and had sworn to himself that no matter what the circumstances, if requested, he would fly his Huey into the heart of hell for them and give it his all anytime the opportunity presented itself. It was a Semper Fi kind of thing with him.

Marine aviation squadrons were designated by the letters VMO. The VMO was followed by a numeral that identified the individual squadrons. Thus, Jim McDonnell's squadron was known as VMO-6. Additionally, each squadron had an identifying name or call sign that they used when communicating with others while on the ground and in flight. An awful lot was expected from the Huey squadrons, and they always answered the call above and beyond all expectations.

Jim McDonnell's squadron, VMO-6, was assigned the call sign, Tundra. This designation was followed by the identification for the individual Huey. Jim's initial Huey had been known as Tundra 7. When lucky Tundra 7 bit the dust, he had been re-assigned to his latest Huey, Tundra 6. The call sign Tundra had been well-known throughout the central highlands of Vietnam before the squadron had moved to their current base much farther south.

The silence of the crew aboard Tundra 6 was in direct contrast to their airborne fighting machine. The engine noise was partially muzzled by engine compartment insulation. In addition, their flight helmets and built-in noise-limiting earphones served the dual purpose of sheltering their eardrums and permitting them to communicate with each other. Despite the constant noise around them, these earphones were their life link to each other.

"Heads up, men! We are now departing the Nam. Welcome to Laos. We will be approaching the landing zone in a few minutes."

As Tundra 6 came into range of the landing zone (LZ), it predictably announced its arrival because of a quirk in the design of the Huey's rotor system. The Huey was designed with only two rotating blades to create its lift. The blade that rotated forward, which was known as the advancing blade, moved at such velocity that the tip of the blade broke the sound barrier and bellowed out a loud *whomp, whomp, whomp* sound that had become a familiar sound to both friend and foe in Southeast Asia. It could be heard far in advance of the Huey's arrival.

The minutes passed quickly, and in the evening twilight, the crew of Tundra 6 could see green smoke below, which indicated the LZ was not hot. No one aboard dared to relax; they all knew matters could change for the worse in the blink of an eye. There was no idle chatter as the intensity aboard the craft heightened. Everyone's jaws tightened. The 60s were ready to rapidly fire their remaining ammo into the LZ. The die had been cast.

Tundra 6 arrived hot and fast. It looked as if it would certainly overshoot the selected landing zone. The small clearing, due to the urgency of the situation, had been haphazardly and hastily selected. It was one of several small clearings that dotted the otherwise overgrown jungle like countryside below them. At first glance, it had appeared to all parties involved to be the least of all evils.

Captain McDonnell knew what he was doing, and because the crew had seen him do this maneuver once before, they hung on for their sorry lives. However, this second time, they welcomed the approach; they all knew the odds and sensed the imminent danger below.

Thus, the combined attitude aboard Tundra 6 was to come in and out, fast and furious. You snooze, you lose. If the recon guys blinked, they would be stuck with their high-value prisoner still in their gripping hands, and the solo Huey would be long gone for home.

However, the guys on the ground knew the game as well as anyone else. They got their package in the door and on the floor of the Huey before the Huey's skids touched the ground. Then, just as fast, both parties reversed direction. The recon marines hustled back into the bush, and the Huey, her crew, and its newly acquired cargo headed back into the perceived safety of the sky. Neither party took a backward glance.

The recon marines were immediately engaged by a superior force that, unknown to them, had been close on their trail. The fatal pause to set up the extraction of their prisoner had permitted the enemy to catch up to them. The recon force exhausted their ammunition in the ensuing firefight and proceeded to engage in hand-to-hand combat with the enemy. They dispatched many of their attackers as they fought to their deaths.

Meanwhile, the Huey groaned as it continued to climb at what seemed to all aboard like a slow climb out of hell. It had a top speed of 125 miles per hour in level flight and was much slower when climbing. Conversely, an enemy rocket-propelled grenade traveled as designed—like a rocket! It wouldn't be an even fight. A single, well-aimed or just damn-lucky shot from an RPG was capable of bringing a Huey to its knees.

The lanky prisoner was bound, gagged, and shaking like Jell-O. He was a tall and rather large man for an Asian, and he was dressed in black pajama garb that was soaked with sweat. His eyes bulged and darted left and then right as he surveyed his precarious predicament. He was scared shitless as he lay bound and shivering on the hard metal floor of the vibrating Huey, where he had been harshly and firmly dumped only seconds before.

The sarge gruffly welcomed him aboard. "If you move, I will throw you out this fucking door." He didn't give a damn if the prisoner understood English or not.

Jim powered the Huey out just as hot as he had taken it in. There was nothing in reserve. He maneuvered the craft defensively. He banked sharply right and then quickly left as he climbed for the hoped-for safety some altitude would bring. The darkness was just about upon them as his copilot set course for the base as they continued to climb.

"Let's go home, men," Jim said.

They all heard that, and there was an onboard sigh of relief from all at the sound of the words. "Roger that," they responded positively.

One hell of a deal, Jim thought to himself.

Going home meant different things to different people, but in that chopper, at that moment, it meant they had made it through another day in the Nam and now Laos. The sand-bagged corrugated steel huts they lived in back at the base would be a welcome sight tonight, along with a few Buds.

With the next breath they took, enemy fire hit them. It blew the entire tail section right off the slowly climbing craft. There was a pronounced shudder as the Huey absorbed the impact. It was a fatal blow to the control system, and the Huey began to gyrate out of control in a rapid spin. The craft and temporarily transfixed crew went around quickly once and then twice as Jim fought with the controls in an attempt to regain some semblance of flight. The crew was immobile and steadfastly pinned by the ensuing centrifugal force.

The engine noise went almost quiet, the out-of-control rotation slowed, and just for a brief moment, time seemed to stop for them all. Then the nose of the Huey dipped straight down toward the on-rushing ground, and the wounded bird lost all characteristics of flight.

Jim urgently looked down to his right and also ahead just as his craft started its downward pitch. They were going down hard, and he knew it. Somewhere down there would be where his fatally crippled craft would make a seat-of-its-ass, fatal uncontrolled crash.

The fractured Huey fell out of the sky like a greased brick. The untold outcome was unfolding all too fast.

"Bad shit, boys!" was all he said.

No one heard him. They were busy taking their last breaths of air, and they knew it. There was no time for hope.

The Huey had been caught in the dead man's curve. The craft was too low and too slow, and all the lift was gone too fast for any type of emergency recovery. They went down hard and fast, smashing nose-down into the trees. Everything plastic cracked and shattered immediately. The tree branches loudly and unmercifully whipped and peeled at the sides as the resulting self-generated wind from the fall blasted in through the open side doors.

The rotors joined in, contributing a lot of damage to the hull and the crew. The spinning rotors turned themselves and the trees to splintering shrapnel. The trees did little to break the fall after the initial contact, and the Huey plunged to the ground and practically self-disintegrated.

The crew and passenger were killed instantly. That fast, they were gone. Some remained in the skeleton of their craft while others were tossed out haphazardly. Their organs were crushed as they absorbed the impact of being tossed first against the trees and then onto the unforgiving ground.

On first impact, Jim— in the most improbable fashion—was thrown forward through the shattered Plexiglas and out of the mangled hulk, followed tightly by the seat into which he was still harnessed. He blindly tumbled toward the ground below; the armored seat shielded him from some of the initial impact with the trees and again when he hit the compact ground.

The jungle's night sounds quickly quieted as the fatally wounded craft crashed uninvited into the anonymous but verbally noisy domain. Abruptly, there was nothing but quiet darkness. Then, after a long tempered pause as the metal intruder gave its final crunching moan, the nocturnal chatter ratcheted up again to exactly where it had curtly left off moments before.

The sounds of the night were in the background as Jim regained consciousness. His flight helmet had been cracked practically in half from impact, and as a result, he had been resoundingly knocked out cold, remaining rigidly embraced by his armored seat.

Suddenly, unannounced, the helicopter's remaining fuel slowly ignited. It sounded off with a warning *whoosh* as it began to brightly betray to the local world the exact location of the fallen craft and its crew. Once again, the night sounds grew silent.

By all accounts, Jim McDonnell might as well have been dead or soon would be, for there were obviously aggressive enemy troops in the immediate area. They would seek out the target of opportunity they had just bulls-eyed, which—by most standards—would be considered a lucky shot.

The bastards that blew them out of the sky would soon see the glowing brightness of the fire and would follow the flame to its source. Then, if necessary, they would finish their task. The burning corpse of the craft had betrayed its final resting place.

Jim tried to clear his vision by rubbing his hand across his eyes. The damn fractured helmet interfered with his hand motion. With some effort, he slowly unfastened the helmet strap from under his bleeding chin. Jimbo's helmet silently bounced once as it came to rest against the face of a body that blindly stared back at him. It was the body of the prized no-name passenger—the son-of-bitch that was responsible for this entire disaster. He momentarily wished he had the opportunity to reach out and kill the bastard.

While mentally trying to review survival tactics, Jim unbuckled himself from his lifesaving seat and slowly rolled himself free of its grip. His slow and painful exit put him face-to-face with his dead companion.

He gradually moved his badly bruised body to a sitting position. He glanced around at his surroundings and then back to the dead prisoner. Nothing and no one was moving. The glow of the flames heightened and expanded his field of view. Another quick glance around was followed by a spinning sensation. Once again, he blacked out.

Chapter 4

His name was Jack Henry Lamont and he was the product of an illicit affair between his Irish mother and a French diplomat she worked for at the French embassy in Ireland. His father never recognized his bastard son but arranged for them to follow him to his next post, which was the French Embassy in Hanoi, Vietnam. Jack's mother worked as a secretary in the embassy.

Jack was basically a bum. He used his father's family name of Lamont only when it pleased or profited him. He had acquired the nickname of Hammering Hank while developing his martial arts skills in Vietnam. The name had stuck.

Hank Lamont was constantly in the mental state of being pissed off. He was a tough, young guy at five foot six and 165 pounds. He had a kick like a mule and a punch to match. Possessing a head of black hair and a darker complexion than a typical Irishman, he was referred to as Black Irish in reference to his distant Spanish ancestry, not intended nor taken to be offensive.

Hank had two major enemies in life. His principal enemy was the Catholic Church. His mother would not marry Lamont because he was not Catholic. She would sleep with him, bear his child, and follow him around the world, but marry him? Never! Hank hated the church. His second scorn was his mother. He could not accept the fact that she would remain a Catholic rather than marry his father. Basically, he was mad at the world but managed to focus on the church and his mother. He hated his mother.

His complex personality complicated his simple life. He eventually enlisted in the French army to avoid some legal complications that were brought about by his short fuse and quick fists. Although too young to serve in the military, his story was supported by his bureaucratic, diplomatic, unacknowledged, and non-caring father, who supplied him with the credentials to pass muster.

The French army was glad to have him. The use of hometown recruits was forbidden by the government to prevent the war from becoming even more unpopular at home. Following some basic training, Hank Lamont was ordered to Dien Bien Phu with the initial detachment of troops. Hank was an angry young man, but he wasn't stupid. It wasn't long before he realized the fatal hopelessness of the situation.

Additionally, he was exasperated that he was one of only a scarce few who felt that way. Hank had a tendency to act on impulse when faced with a decision. Consequences never mattered much to him, and consequently he looked for a way out of the impending doom.

On March 13, 1954, as both sides ostensibly readied for peace talks in Geneva, the French selected a location known as Dien Bien Phu as a site for a showdown battle with the Viet Minh. Politically, the French needed a major victory to break the existing stalemate and enhance their position at the peace talks. Continuing to fight a guerilla-style war was not in their best interests.

They believed this was a last-ditch best chance to end an extremely frustrating eight-year guerrilla jungle war with something other than total capitulation at the peace table in Geneva.

Dien Bien Phu was a quaint tribal village situated on the Nam Yum River. The French had built an airfield in the ten-mile long, six-mile wide valley. They built fortifications called firebases on eight hills surrounding the airfield. Later it was footnoted that the hills were named after the French commander in chief, General Henri Navarre's former mistresses. It has been documented that the French general also sent a written challenge to the enemy commander, General Giap.

Inside the hastily built fortress, which was geographically located at the outer limits of the range of their air power, the French built a series of fortified bunkers. They positioned their artillery in the open so they could fire in all directions. The fortress and the firebases were manned by approximately fifteen thousand regular soldiers and legionnaires of various nationalities. They were under the command of Brigadier General Christian de la Croix de Castries.

Not long after the establishment of the base, two 10,000-man divisions under command of General Vo Nguyen Giap surrounded Dien Bien

Phu. A third division bypassed the fortress and attacked into Laos. By December, Indochina was cut in half.

The Viet Minh had dutifully managed to portage more than two hundred artillery pieces, anti-aircraft guns, and unknown numbers of Russian-made rocket launchers through heavily jungle like terrain previously dismissed by the French as totally impassable.

In short order, the firebases were overrun one by one, and the airstrip was systematically destroyed. All the while, a constant shelling of the French ensued. The artillery duel was extremely one-sided as the French guns, which had been placed in the open, were destroyed.

The monsoon season arrived and resupply by air evaporated. The French troops began to starve and died at an alarming rate. Over five thousand men were severely wounded out of an initial total of fifteen thousand.

The French General discussed a breakout versus surrender with his superior in Hanoi. Both options were dismissed in favor of fighting to the end, but with one proviso—the men in Isabelle, the southernmost strongpoint closest to the jungle, and the closest to friendly forces in Laos should be given a chance to make a break for it. Approximately seventy men from Isabelle made good on their escape.

In the end, the entire fortress was overrun, and ten thousand survivors surrendered. Again, unknown by many today, these troops began a torturous death march to the Viet Minh prison camps over three hundred miles to the east. Unlike the Bataan death march of WWII, very few of the ten thousand soldiers survived.

The outcome of that battle would determine the future of the French military presence in Vietnam and open the door to the quagmire into which the American military eventually entered.

An unknown number of the seventy soldiers from Isabelle survived. However, one such survivor was a sixteen-year-old legionnaire who had lied about his age and background in order to join the military.

When the remaining force at firebase Isabelle was given the option of fighting to the death or risking capture versus making a break for it into the jungle towards Laos, Hank immediately opted for the latter. At the appointed hour, he was gone and was one of the few that eventually met up with the friendly forces in Laos. He didn't know it at the time but he was about to make a decision that would put him on a collision course with Jim McDonnell.

Hank elected to remain in Laos. He dropped out of society as he had known it; in reality, he really had no place to go. He and a fellow escapee traveled south through Laos on a main trail and eventually, after a long journey, stopped rather than cross over the southern Laotian border with Vietnam to the east and Cambodia to the southwest.

Chapter 5

This area of Laos was known as Attapeu Province. The capital city, also named Attapeu, was located several kilos east of the main north-south trail, in a valley surrounded by low mountains. Attapeu's indigenous people were distrustful of outsiders. The Laotians in the south considered the natives wild and unpredictable and thus avoided the area.

The prevailing religious practices in Attapeu consisted of a form of spiritualism and black magic, which was used to deal with any dangerous sprits that arose in their village or the surrounding mountains. The native population was sparse and made up of various ethnic groups that existed on the margins of society. Other provinces traditionally viewed them as uncivilized. They lived off the forest on swidden cultivation rather than rice paddy cultivation.

Hong Tre, known as the quiet place, was a small gathering of seven stilted huts. This quiet settlement was located a stone's throw east of the city of Attapeu. It was a relatively new settlement on an ancient east-west trail that led from the border of South Vietnam across the major north-south trail that Hank had traveled and continued westward. Hank's southward path of travel was later to become known as the Ho Chi Minh trail. The east-west trail passed directly through the settlement of Hong Tre and the city of Attapeu. It continued across Laos and into the southern part of Cambodia.

Hong Tre had no history. Although considered permanent by its inhabitants, it was not known outside the area and did not appear on any maps. Hong Tre was initially settled around 1950 by several Laotian families who had numerous children. They had migrated from the lowlands, seeking refuge from the French influence in their area. The locals in the nearby town of Attapeu tolerated their intrusion and a live-and-let-live attitude had prevailed.

Hank eventually stumbled into their midst one day in 1954, along with a fellow survivor from the Isabelle garrison. Their southward journey had extended over ten months. They were both at the end of their ropes, and the natives took them in with no questions asked but with some reservations.

The "outsiders" were joined in 1966 by a quiet fellow who claimed to be of Cambodian decent. He pitched in with the forest cultivating and harvesting. For some unspoken reason, he appeared to be on the run, so to speak. He announced his name as Trang Rath. He spoke several Asian languages, and he also spoke extremely good English. This fact he kept to himself.

The people of Attapeu and Hong Tre permitted all three outsiders' seemingly harmless intrusions, cautiously observed their odd mannerisms, and eventually accepted them as neighbors. Over time, they proved to be good neighbors and quite trustworthy. Additionally, they more than pulled their own weight to help sustain daily life in the settlement. They seldom, if ever, ventured into Attapeu.

Travelers no longer used the trail. No one wanted to travel into Vietnam due to the war, and the only ones coming out were deserters from both sides. Very few of them survived in the bush, and none had ever made it to Hong Tre.

****

As time went by, Hank's darker side took over his mindset. Although not a single individual had visited their settlement since his arrival a little over eleven years earlier, Hank had begun to feel the need to be heavily armed in order to protect himself and his home. He had a sense that the unwelcome war in Vietnam was drawing closer and closer to them. It was now 1967.

Hank and Trang Rath had developed a trusting relationship. Trang mostly kept to himself and played everything close to the vest. He spoke to Hank in French and occasional Vietnamese. Trang also shared that he understood and spoke English, and they often communicated in English as Hank, for some unspoken reason, wished to improve his English skills.

Whenever any essentials were needed by the settlement, Trang always came up with the francs for one of the others to go into Attapeu to make the necessary purchase. The others respected him for his generosity in their otherwise cashless society. Gestures such as this would eventually lead to his discovery.

Hank's fellow survivor from Dien Bien Phu was not quite as paranoid as Hank. Hayrack Algiers had been eighteen years old, two years Hank's senior, when they had met up at Dien Bien Phu. Hayrack was Algerian and had been a new member of the French foreign legion. Hank and Hayrack had quickly formed a bond while under fire in the hellhole of Dien Bien Phu, and each had admired the other's willingness to fight like hell while others alongside them cowered. They had also seen the futility of it all early on.

Hayrack was uneducated and worldly. He had joined the legion a year earlier while in Algiers. It hadn't taken him long to get himself into trouble, and he was soon on his way to Vietnam.

On several occasions in the past, Hank and Hayrack had suppressed the urge to flee farther west to distance themselves from the war in Vietnam. However, they had both subconsciously grown fond of their neighbors and outwardly fond of two of their neighbors' daughters. Six years earlier, Hank and Hayrack married the younger women in a brief ceremony, followed by a daylong celebration, and now each had two beautiful children. Hank's oldest boy was five, and the other was three. Hayrack had a daughter and a son that were about the same age as Hank's children. Life was sweet.

Hank was most comfortable in his surroundings. No one ever gave him an order. No one ever told him what to do or when to do it. He often thought to himself and verbalized to his two friends, "No one will ever find me here, and if they do, I will kill them."

Hayrack believed, rightfully so, that Hank was losing his mind. The village was totally indefensible, and if the war spread farther into Laos, Hayrack planned to pick up his family and just move farther west. He began to distance himself from the others. His mental plan was that he would stay ahead of the expanding hostilities by moving westward until it chased him into a major city, where his fate would be sealed for he could no longer even comprehend living among the masses.

This was his dilemma. It began to weigh heavily on his mind, and the question reverberated in his head: Should I stay or should I go? And if I go, then when?

After more than a decade of ignorant bliss, the activity along the Ho Chi Minh trail had heightened in its intensity, thanks to the Americans. Daytime bombings had intensified, and exploding bombs could be increasingly heard in the distance from Hong Tre.

The nighttime movement of Viet Minh troops to the south had now become the norm. Hank was convinced it was only a matter of time before the Americans would bomb the trail day and night and possibly even invade Laos to completely disrupt the activity on the trail.

Chapter 6

In 1959, a series of ancient trails running south within Laos were formalized into a "special trail" to support the war in South Vietnam. The Laotian government was engaged in a war against the Pathet Lao in the northern part of Laos and was unable to stop the use of its territory.

The Truong Son Strategic Supply Route was named after the long mountain chain that separated Vietnam from Laos. It had its beginning in Vinh, which was located in southern North Vietnam. In addition to its official name, the trail later became known by its American name, the Ho Chi Minh trail.

West of Vinh and just north of the demilitarized zone were three mountain passes that led directly to Laos. It was in this area of Laos that the trail began to run south. The trail went south through eastern Laos for several hundred miles. Along the way, various mountain passes were used to gain access to South Vietnam.

The North Vietnamese launched a huge project to upgrade the trail for use by trucks in 1964. In 1965, the United States began its secret war in Laos. It lasted for four years and became a political issue in 1969. American troops killed in Laos were listed as "killed in Southeast Asia." Later in 1971, with the Americans troops withdrawn, the South Vietnamese army with American advisors re-entered Laos. They were supported by American air power.

Much of Hank's information about the war came from grilling an occasional stray trooper he would pick up on the trail. His understanding of Vietnamese was beyond pretty good, and his ability to speak the language hovered around not so bad. When he finished gleaning information, he dispatched these stray victims and carefully disposed of the bodies before fading back into the bush.

Thus, he magnified the evening forays into the bush for military supplies. Hank knew his way up and down the trail for several kilos. He had visited it many times in the past to observe the sporadic activity along it. As part of his haphazard survival plan, he had established a secure hiding place for his stash of weapons, just one hundred yards north of his hut in Hong Tre. He selected an area that he could quickly reach, where the tree line met the open field that led from his living area. He had established a straight line pathway directly from his hut to the buried bunker, where he had amassed a mixture of AK-47s and RPGs. Additionally, he mined the hell out of the open field and also mined a selected section of his well-worn pathway that led from Hong Tre to the Ho Chi Minh trail.

Everyone in the settlement was aware of the mines and steadfastly avoided the area. Trang and Hayrack were the only others that knew their way through the mined pathway. They had to trust that Hank would not alter the layout of the mines, and thus they—like the others—never ventured into the area of the bunker without Hank being present.

One particular evening, Hank had staked out an area of the trail like a tiger waiting for the prey to fall out of the protection of the herd. He would strike swiftly and silently, drag his prey into the bush, and strip them of any information, weapons, and ammo they might be carrying. His goal was to continually build up an arsenal with which to protect himself, his family, and the settlement that had become a permanent home to him.

Hong Tre was only a kilo or so from where Jim McDonnell's Huey crashed and burned. By chance that evening, Hank had stealthy staked out a position along the trail that was in close proximity to what would become the fateful crash site.

As was his practice, Hank was positioned to take advantage of any straggler that happened to fall out of rank from the steady stream of southbound reinforcements of fighting men and women. He really didn't need their meager supplies of rice; rather to kill and acquire an occasional AK-47 or RPG launcher, along with ammunition and some information, made it a night of good hunting.

This night, the sound of the crash alerted him. The glow of the fire quickly brought him to the site to search for any contraband he could gather. He knew those on the trail would not dare break ranks and leave the trail to investigate. At the same time, he was sure there were ground forces also hustling toward the flames, thirsting to finish off any survivors.

Hank arrived ahead of all others. Upon seeing the extent of the wreckage and the advanced stage of the fire—the pale green aluminum skin of the helicopter had begun to melt off its twisted skeleton—he knew there was nothing left to salvage. While surveying the rest of the site, he tripped over the dead Asian captive and landed squarely on top of Jim McDonnell. He immediately realized the fallen stranger had been one of the pilots; he was also breathing and still had some life left in him.

At the same moment, Jim came to once again, and their startled stares silently met. They could both see the telltale flames from the burning fuel dancing in each other's eyes.

"American, can you walk?" Hank asked.

It sounded to Jim as if someone was speaking to him in an echoing voice. He heard the words twice, if not three times. He broke eye contact and began to shake his head as if to dump out the echo. Then, in a rough whisper he muttered a response, "Yeah, I think so. Hope so."

Hank placed his arms under Jim's in an attempt to help him to his feet. Once up, Jim placed his hands on Hank's shoulders to steady himself.

"Thanks." His reply was raspy and all he could utter as he grappled for balance.

Hank eyed him suspiciously. He quickly weighed the pros and cons of helping this poor bastard get the hell out of dodge or sticking a blade in him, gutting him, and leaving him for dead.

Dead men tell no tales, he thought. *On the other hand, I could really use some new company.* Hank had just finished his inner dialogue when Jim seemed to gain his sea legs. Hank knew he had to act fast; the dogged pursuers would soon be upon them.

"Who is the one in black?" Hank asked.

Jim stammered the answer. "A prisoner … Our captive … We just picked him up."

Perfect! Hank thought to himself. He immediately formed a scheme. Almost unconsciously, he slipped the dog tags off over Jim's head and, bending to the ground, rapidly placed them around the neck of the dead Vietnamese prisoner.

"Strip out of your flight suit," Hank barked.

"Shouldn't we be getting the hell out of here?" Jim protested. His instincts told him to run like hell.

"*Oui, mon ami,*" Hank said without looking up at Jim. He continued, "They all know how many are in your crew. If the count doesn't add up, they will come looking for survivors. You must trust me."

31

Hank felt elevated about his act of deception as he watched Jim boldly but with much anguish comply with his brisk request. Jim quickly stripped and dumped the flight suit. Hank hurriedly relieved the cadaver of its two-piece black pajama attire and tossed it to Jim. He then substituted the flight suit for the black tatter. For good measure, he placed the broken flight helmet on the dead man's head. The odd couple immediately left the scene with Jim, sporting his new black garb, closely following Hank into the bush.

They headed almost two kilos farther into Laos and the relative safety of Hong Tre. Jim eventually had no memory of any of these occurrences. In fact, his entire past historical memory was wiped blank. His memory vault was empty. This total void was a direct result of the shock of the head trauma he had suffered.

He moved at a quick pace in a westerly direction, trying desperately to keep up with Hank. It became obvious that Hank knew exactly where he was headed and that he intended to arrive there in one piece. How his traveling companion arrived was left entirely up to him and his physical and mental stamina. Jim was determined to be up to the task.

He was about to start a new life, completely removed from everything and everyone he had ever known. Although not immediately aware of his condition, he would lose all recall of his past life. For now, he was very much alive and extremely grateful to his rescuer. He stayed in the man's shadow all the way to the village. They arrived silently in the darkness.

Jim felt that they were being watched. The hair on his neck rose cautiously, as did all his survival instincts. He reached out and touched Hank on the back to get his attention.

"Quiet now," Hank turned and whispered as he continued forward. "My friend Hayrack is only expecting one person. As two, we could become his targets. Stay close to me now. We are going to leave the trail for a short distance."

Jim didn't ask the reason for the diversion, but Hank continued speaking, "I have mined the trail up ahead. You best remember that."

Jim's reply was a nod of his head as he wondered how the hell he would ever again find this particular spot on the trail into the settlement. He rationalized that that would be the least of his concerns. He began to feel poorly and staggered to one knee. He clasped his hands to his head while the realization that he was gradually losing awareness crept over him.

This is it! he thought. His life was draining out of him on a half-assed, unknown jungle pathway in bumfuck Laos. One way or the other, he was on the way out, either from his head injuries or at the hand of some freaking Frenchman. His last conscious thought was, *It's a damn lousy deal.*

Chapter 7

It had been cooler than usual the night before, and a light mist had formed on the river and now slowly moved over the open field around the settlement. The onset of daylight brought the rays of sun that would quickly burn off the mist as though it never happened. And with another cool evening to follow, the mist would return the next morning.

Thus began the cycle of activity in the settlement. Everyone went about their daily activities, sans Jim McDonnell, and this cycle would repeat day after day. His cycle moved from semi-conscious to unconscious since his total collapse on the trail the night before.

Time passed, and days turned into weeks. The seasonal weather was mild, and the bombing noise from the trail was unusually quiet. There was much talk about the new stranger that was living with Hank and his family, but other than Hank and his wife, no adults in the settlement had had any contact with him up to this point.

It was now the beginning of May, and the monsoon season would soon be upon them. Jim was back on his feet. He had been in and out of consciousness and had survived on water and some occasional nibbles of fish and a daily swallow of rice.

On this particular uneventful late afternoon, Jim stooped in the low open doorway of Hank's hut. He looked outward toward the river and observed the locals. He spotted Hank sitting nearby with his wife and family and decided to approach Hank and ask some questions that had begun to churn around rather piecemeal in his mind. Although still very weak, he was full of questions and had grown impatient with the previous lack of answers forthcoming from Hank. As he approached, Hank motioned for his family to leave them alone.

Jim smiled as he met Hank's eyes and slowly sat down opposite him on a worn woven matt. His motion was slow and deliberate, and as he comfortably positioned himself on the mat, he began to speak. "Hank, I'm tired of having you tell me nothing about how you found me. I appreciate your hospitality—" He stopped abruptly and took a long look about the settlement. "I truly do appreciate everything you have done for me. Now I need to know some details. I have no idea who I am, what my background is, or for that matter, where the hell I am. You say we're in Laos, and I ask, how the hell did I get here?"

Hank was not overly thrilled to have this long overdue conversation. Some of his neighbors—notably Hayrack and Trang—had distanced themselves from him as of late. Trang had made an effort to warm up to Jim, but Hayrack would have nothing to do with him. He felt, like many of the others, that Jim's presence was a bad omen. It bothered Hank that they would dwell on the subject of the "bad omen," but he didn't share his sense of foreboding about the war that was surely coming their way.

Now on top of that concern, he had to deal with some less-than-delicate probing from Jim that he would just as soon have avoided. He would have much rather enjoyed some lighter conversation about the coming change in the weather, but Jim's demeanor indicated that the anticipated questions could no longer be avoided.

"As I told you, your name is Jim. I found you in the jungle and thought you were dead."

Hank had said this much before, and he damn well knew it would not suffice any longer. He wrestled with the truth. His thought was that if the truth came out, Jim would wish to leave and attempt to return to the Americans. Hank determined that such a journey, if undertaken, would be suicidal. Even worse would be for Jim to be taken captive and forced to tell of the existence of Hong Tre. Thus, under no circumstances would Jim be allowed to leave Hong Tre alive.

"Jim, I can only tell you what I know, but you must be prepared to accept the truth from me even if you find it extremely difficult to swallow. You must also refrain from any impulsive actions that could bring you or us any harm."

"Listen up, Hank! Let's get something straight between us." Jim spoke more firmly now. He did not want this conversation to follow the paths of several other such inquiries that had gone in circles and had eventually led nowhere. "Any goddamn thing you give me would be much better than the void I feel. Right now, I am no one. My life is a blank to me. Jesus Christ, man, just tell me everything you know, and tell me now."

Then he did it. Hank quickly weighed his options. He didn't want to lose this soldier. He desperately wanted his company, for he knew unknown change was on the horizon. He felt strongly that he needed the strength he sensed in this man—the man whose life he had saved on the trail and nursed back to health here in the settlement. He looked Jim directly in the eyes and spoke up boldly as he deliberately but delicately told Jim a selfish lie.

"Jim, as best I can tell, you are a deserter from the American military." Hank immediately went quiet as he lowered his eyes and glanced away from Jim.

Jim sat quietly absorbing the low-key, non-emotional response to his probe. He attempted to search his empty memory for some clue that would help him verify what Hank had just told him.

A deserter? he asked himself before seeking clarification from Hank. How could this be without him knowing it? How could this possibly be? "Hank, I need details. What more do you know?" What Hank had just told him went against everything his mind could fathom at the time.

Hank hastily gathered himself and continued, "Jim, I found you in the bush near the trail, half-dead. You are obviously an American, but you were wearing peasant clothing, and you had no identification. You were armed with a pistol, and thus it was clear to me that you were not an escaped prisoner. Besides, you were in Laos. There are no Americans in Laos. I put it together and determined that you must have been on the run, so to speak. When I asked you your name, you mumbled something to me that I could not understand, and then you told me it was Jungle Jim. That was all I was able to get from you."

"How the hell did I lose my memory?"

"I do not know, my friend. Perhaps over time your mind will heal itself. Until then, we are here inside Laos, where I am concerned our safety is in jeopardy."

"Jeopardy?"

Hank's statement momentarily moved Jim off of the subject at hand, and Hank took his leave. Later in the day, Hank and Jim gathered for some lighter conversation, but Jim digressed and returned to the weighty subject of their earlier conversation, though not for long.

The sun moved behind the treetops, and the usual quiet end of the day activities began to unfold around the settlement. As Hank and Jim sat in silence, digesting the dourness of their conversation, they observed two individuals walking toward them from the direction of nearby Attapeu. This was a rather rare sight for all and a somewhat alarming sight for Hank. The others in the settlement had already discreetly disappeared out of sight.

The two strangers seemed to zero in on Hank and Jim where they both sat in silent observation.

"Stay seated here. I'll return briefly." Hank rose while speaking and casually walked over to his hut. When he reached the entrance, he glanced back with a quick look, stooped low, and then disappeared into the darkened opening.

Jim gave him a surprised parting glance and then quickly returned his attention to the approaching strangers. The sun was at their backs, and it took a moment for Jim to determine that they were indeed as focused on him as he was on them.

The taller of the two raised a friendly hand as both individuals left the trail and started to close the space between themselves and where Jim was sitting. When they were within a comfortable but unthreatening distance, the tall one spoke up as they both stopped in their tracks. "English? Australian? Possibly American?"

Jim didn't take the bait, and he continued to eye them as they again started to close the distance separating them from him. After moving closer, they stopped within ten feet or so, as if waiting for a verbal selection to their multiple choice question and an invitation to approach further to a more friendly distance for conversation.

The second of the two strangers was Asian, and he did nothing but stare curiously at Jim. The taller, more verbal one was possibly American. Their attire, though sweaty, was suited for the environment and a little more upscale than Jim had seen lately. They both wore a khaki variation of what Jim knew as a bush jacket. He also knew they were both probably armed.

Jim elected to not answer the question, but he did gesture for them to sit and join him. He positioned them so they would be looking directly into the setting sun. The two alighted cautiously.

Jim's heart was pounding. *Where the hell is Hank?* he thought as he looked around to find not a single soul from the settlement in sight. He marveled at the smoothness of the settlement drill. Everyone had quietly scattered into their huts at the approach of the two strangers. He returned his attention to the two now-seated, uninvited visitors.

"*Mon ami*. I see we have company," Hank proffered a friendly French greeting and offered no reason for his sudden departure only moments before. He resettled himself on the mat next to Jim, opposite the two visitors, who were now comfortably seated.

Hank was much more relaxed upon his return than he had been during his brief departure. Of course, now he was armed; he had Jim's loaded sidearm hidden at his side. He was additionally relieved that neither of the two strangers appeared to be armed, but he was wrong on that account.

Once again, the taller of the two strangers inquired of Jim in English, "So, as I asked, are you English, American, or Australian?"

"Why do you ask?" Jim replied with a broad smile that told his questioner there would be no immediate answer to the query. This response didn't appear to faze either of the outsiders. They were obviously aware of the private nature of the people in this area. However, Jim's presence here had really piqued their interest.

They could boil me in oil and I still couldn't tell them a damn thing, Jim thought.

Hank sarcastically joined in with a question of his own in English. "Gentlemen, what brings you to our settlement this fine day?"

The sun was a little lower now, and it became necessary for the visitors to shade their eyes as they maintained eye contact with their hosts. Jim unconsciously placed a moniker—the sunshine boys—on the squinting strangers as they responded to Hank's question by getting right to the point of their unannounced visit.

"Actually, we are looking for someone who might be in this area or may have passed through here recently," the Asian guest spoke up and then continued in perfect English, not waiting for an answer. "It is quite unusual for us to have a conversation in English in these parts. I find it quite refreshing."

Hank, ignoring the last statement, responded to the question in a concerned manner, using his best English. "What is the name of the individual you are looking for, and should we be concerned for our safety?" His question was direct, and if the two men wanted to maintain decorum, it required a direct answer.

The tall one spoke first. He carefully responded, "He is going by the name Trang Rath."

The Asian, now slightly piqued by Hank's manner, spoke up in English, adding a slight grit to his words. "The name is Trang Rath, though that is not his given name. He is a Cambodian, and no, his presence would not present anyone with any reason for concern. He is just an old acquaintance of ours who has, shall we say, strayed from our *company*, and we wish him to return."

CIA no doubt, Jim thought.

That damn Trang, Hank thought. *What the hell is he running from?*

Jim broke the silence. "We have been here for many years, and I don't believe we have ever seen any strangers from Cambodia. We really never have anyone come through here anymore."

The two strangers stiffened slightly as Jim finished his lie, for they had previously asked around in Attapeu and had been informed otherwise.

Hank followed with a quick question of his own in English, "Is there some type of gratuity available if one were to find your associate or at the least supply information where one might find him?" Hank finished his question and sat back to await their answer. He also positioned himself so as to easily produce his weapon if it became necessary.

Looking first to Jim and then to Hank, the Asian responded, "Mister, this is Southeast Asia. There is always money to be put on the table for the right information."

His tall partner elaborated on the offer. "Would American dollars or francs be acceptable?"

It became patently obvious that these two strangers didn't intend to play around, but they were both willing to play along, at least for now. They had no idea Trang was figuratively right under their snooping noses, but the good-cop-bad-cop routine that had just played out before them by their hosts sent them a positive message. Or so they assumed.

Jim picked up on Hank's cooperative feint and offered what he felt was a positive question. "How long will you be in the area?" Neither he nor Hank were disappointed with the resulting change in their guests' body language and the Asian's almost instant response.

The two strangers immediately relaxed their posture and seemed to somewhat lighten up. They looked toward each other, and then the Asian responded in a low-key, almost friendly manner. "We will be in Attapeu through tonight and most of tomorrow if necessary. Our ride will arrive in the morning. Will this give you enough time to arrange something?"

"Yes!" Hank's rapid response sealed the end of the conversation.

"Shall we return or will you come to us?"

Jim had what he thought would be the last words. "Why don't you both drop by around midmorning before the sun gets too high overhead?"

The invitation was extended and accepted without another word. Jim and Hank stood up, and the two strangers followed suit. They exchanged mutually brief nods, and as the strangers turned to part, Hank pointedly remarked, "Francs. We prefer payment in francs."

Without offering the slightest response, the strangers retraced their steps back toward the pathway as Jim turned to Hank. He silently asked with his outstretched hands and then added verbally, "What in the hell just took place here?"

Hank shrugged. He smiled a wry smile and raised his eyebrows. "Don't really know, but it seemed like the right thing to do. Those guys must know Trang is here. Let's go inside and talk this over. I'll round up Trang, and we can bring him up to speed on the conversation. The three of us will surely be able to come up with a plan. Worst case, we shoot the bastards and take their money."

Jim nervously observed that Hank was obviously not joking, and he began to have a bad feeling about how things would unfold the next day. The sun finally set as Jim sat to one side in the comfort of the hut that had become his temporary home. Hank asked his wife to take the children and accompany him to Hayrack's hut.

While waiting patiently alone for Hank to return with Trang, Jim began thinking about whether the situation was an opportunity or a mine field. He had much to wonder but not long to wait. Hank's wife and children remained with Hayrack and his family while the ensuing three-way conversation brought Trang up to speed about the two strangers inquiring about his presence. Once Hank and Jim finished, Trang exhaled heavily and proceeded to cautiously share his background with them, at which point it became a one-way conversation.

First he explained that Trang Rath was not his given name. He was an American, born to a Catholic mother of Cambodian decent and a Wall Street WASP father. He was well educated, and his family was rather well-to-do and extremely well-known in American political circles.

He lightly brushed past his educational credentials with a quick reference to his Ivy League business degree from Yale and his employment on Wall Street as a savvy up-and-coming international banker. He purposely skipped any other mention of his family and fast-forwarded to the past several years.

After stumbling over his words about a failed romance, he stated that he had abruptly dropped out of his social and economic life. He eventually left the States as a Christian missionary and sometime thereafter ended up in Northern Laos. Neither Hank nor Jim pressed him for additional details. They were both extremely impatient for him to get to the end of the story.

Trang finally got to the here and now. It was here in northern Laos that, through a series of circumstances, he had been unconsciously drawn into the struggle between the Laotian government and the Communist Pathet Lao. He again purposely shortened his tale by highlighting his two-year involvement assisting the CIA with humanitarian efforts in supplying the Hmong tribal people with basic living necessities.

This support had led to him becoming friendly with the Laotian military leaders at various locations in the mountainous regions surrounding the Plain of Jars in northern Laos. His efforts on their behalf and their interest in him had spun completely out of his control. He skipped more details and gave broad brush strokes to the clandestine efforts of the Laotian brass to use locally grown opium as a medium to feed their insatiable financial appetite.

Trang stopped speaking and looked directly at the both of them. Then he sincerely stated, "The more you know, the greater your risk. Earlier today, I discretely observed the two that have come for me. I briefly met them up north, and I don't believe they will permit you to live to tell this story."

Jim nodded to himself. His guess had been on-target. They were CIA all right. Hank had no fear of anyone who walked the face of the earth. He had become extremely hardened by his experiences, and he harbored a take-no-prisoners attitude toward life and his fellow man, present company excluded—at least for now.

The two strangers were, in Hank's words, "ordinary everyday assholes." He continued to question Trang. "Tell us all you can, and let the chips fall where they may. But first, tell us your given American name."

Trang sighed at Hank's bravado and looked toward Jim to assess his position on this delicate and possibly life-altering situation. He didn't have to take more than a breath to know where Jim stood.

Jim responded. "I'm all in, Trang. Now, what is your name, and what is the rest of the story?"

Trang lowered his head, and ever so slowly and softly, he inhaled deeply. Then with a partial exhale followed by a sorrowful pause, he continued. "I'm truly sorry to have brought this predicament into our midst. I fear things will now never be the same for us here. If I flee, or in fact if we all just disappear into the bush tonight, they will follow, and in doing so, they will leave a path of destruction behind in Hong Tre."

Jim began to wonder if Trang's travels had brought him to the point of paranoia.

Trang continued, "You only saw two of them, but there are many others available to follow up if necessary. You cannot mix it up with these guys and come out on top. I will give myself up to them tomorrow upon their return. This will buy you, at best, a day or two. Trust me. They are deadly, vindictive pricks, and they will return—probably with helicopter gunships—and level the entire settlement. Gentlemen, we have our own little Catch 22."

Jim's questioning of Trang's mental condition heightened with each elaboration Trang proclaimed. The familiar sound of the bombing on the trail started in the distance. The rolling thunder indicated that the Americans were bombing somewhere to the north and would progressively fly southward and methodically pockmark everything beneath them. The activity had become so common that the three men hardly noticed the now overly familiar white noise of the bombing.

A pause for a deep breath did nothing to disturb the now tomblike stillness in their circle. Trang abruptly broke the silence. "My name is Thatcher Pittsford. Thatch is what I prefer. Shall I go on?"

"We're not going anywhere tonight, Thatch. So yes, tell us more. Possibly we can come up with some type of plan to resolve our predicament by dawn," Jim said.

Hank looked in awe at Jim as he finished speaking. He was astonished by Jim's air of naïveté. If Hank had his way, he would charge into Attapeu this very night, find the two shits, kill them in their sleep, and let the other shoe hit the bloody floor when and where it may. However, he felt his plan could wait awhile, possibly until early dawn at the latest. For now, he would sit back and just listen to Thatch.

"General Ptope was *the* big man in the Laotian army, and he was running the show in northern Laos. I had become very friendly with the general, and one day out of the blue, he arranged for me to meet with another officer, a colonel that was his right-hand man. We met at the Paradise Hotel in downtown Udon."

Jim once again interrupted. "Udon, Thatch? What or where is Udon?"

"Udon is in northern Thailand, just south of the Laos border. There, in the middle of nowhere, sits a small town known as Udon Thani and a huge airbase that is known as Udorn. Believe it or not, Udorn is one of the busiest airports in the world. I'll tell you more about Udorn some other time." Thatch paused momentarily and surveyed the room. He hoped the magnitude of his story, now that he was finally telling it, was being totally absorbed by his two friends.

Hank, who was sitting cross-legged on the floor, impatiently motioned toward Thatch with outstretched, up-turned hands. He waved his fingers toward himself, indicating he wished Thatch to end the delay and continue with his dialogue.

"During our meeting at the hotel, the colonel relayed what he wished me to do and exactly when I was to commence doing it. I was to arrange banking accommodations for a regular flow of large monetary deposits and ensuing wire transfers of such funds to discreet banking institutions in the Cayman Islands."

Thatch assumed Hank and Jim were familiar with these banking locations and continued, "The colonel and I drove over to the air base where an Air America Beechcraft was waiting for me on the tarmac. He told me everything was arranged by W.B. Coade, the CIA agent-in-charge of Laotian OPS. It was arranged for me to travel to Bangkok via Air America and then by a commercial airline on to Malaysia. In Malaysia, I was to communicate electronically to make the necessary arrangements in the Cayman Islands and then return to Bangkok and catch an Air America ride back to Udorn."

Another brief pause was followed by a gulp of fresh breath. "The transactions were to commence directly upon my return with the necessary account numbers. The accounts were for the general of the regional Laotian forces and this aforementioned colonel that was his direct report." Thatch continued, "These two men are very powerful and evil. This money was to be paid in return for the outflow of like quantities of heroin. How that was and is occurring is the heart of another story, which has no bearing on us here and now. A share of the money goes to finance a lavish lifestyle for these two jackals, and the share which is reverently referred to as retirement money was to go to the numbered accounts."

Another deep breath by Thatch was followed by total silence. Not one member of the gathered group uttered a syllable. The bombing continued in the distance, but it was moving closer and growing louder. "Still want to know more?"

Jim asked a quick question. "Thatch, are you saying that the head CIA guy in northern Laos is involved in this illicit undertaking?"

"No, I'm not. He is, I think, above reproach. But well, you know, he just doesn't give a damn about what the general and his ilk do on their own time as long as the military job gets done. So when he is asked by the jackals to arrange things such as my flights to open the accounts, no questions are asked. Things just get done. I doubt he knew or cared about the nature of my undertaking."

Jim responded with a slow nod of the head, his face pale. "Go ahead, Thatch, continue. Sorry to interrupt."

"I set up the accounts as directed and returned to Bangkok as planned. Once I arrived there, I made the decision to bolt. My reason, you might ask? Who the hell knows? It could possibly have been a guilty conscience, possibly a lack of balls, or probably a combination of the two. Who the hell knows what motivated me to act. However, I will tell you this: while I was airborne on the return trip and approaching Bangkok, a question entered my mind. What would the general need me for once I gave him the newly established bank account information?

"That question began to eat at me, and I had a few drinks in me, so when my commercial flight landed in Bangkok, instead of meeting an Air America plane for the planned return flight to Udorn, I caught a commercial flight to Phonm Phen, Cambodia." Thatch stopped as if he was waiting for his words to catch up to him; it seemed almost as though he himself was having trouble comprehending his own actions.

Hank and Jim exchanged wide-eyed glances and quickly returned their focus to Thatch as he continued. "From Phonm Phen, I disappeared into the countryside. Although I'm a bit tall, as you can tell, I resemble my mother more than my father; thus, until now, I have moved across the country relatively unnoticed. Now, these two guys—our visitors—must surely want the banking information I have, and now that I'm processing this whole scenario, hopefully their orders are to deliver me back alive. As for you and your family and friends, I'm afraid your future is bleak now that they know I am living among you."

The inordinate amount of time spent in the telling of Thatch's story had brought them much closer to dawn than any of them realized. Suddenly, without sharing his feelings, Hank had heard enough and decided it was time to act. He was not going to die with his boots off. No, it would be the two strangers who would be caught napping.

"I'm going to get Hayrack. Wait here for me."

Jim and Thatch were both sitting silently, mentally exhausted when Hank returned shortly with a sleepy Hayrack. He hastily addressed the now-assembled group of four. Still on his feet as Hayrack sank to the floor, Hank barked out a command. "There is no time to explain. You will all follow me, *now.*"

The others, after a brief bewildered hesitation, rose to their feet and prepared to follow Hank's order. Hank led them out of the hut, around to the rear of the structure, and on to the path that snaked out toward the tree line where the fortified bunker containing his confiscated weapons was located. It was not yet light out, and the path was ill defined in the low light of the approaching dawn.

"Stay in line directly behind me, and do not stray off the path," Hank warned.

There was intensity in Hank's voice and manner as he set a fast pace to the bunker. His plan was for them to arm themselves, go into Attapeu, and wipe up the floor with the two strangers and anyone else that dared to interfere with them. Hank had formulated a paranoia-fueled plan, and anyone who failed to accept the invitation to join in once he announced it would fall exactly on the spot where they had elected to decline. It seemed that Hank had finally gone round the bend and that Thatch was closely following in his shadow.

It appeared to Jim that Hank was about to take the lead in a mad race to escape reality. To Jim, the situation did not seem to be as dour as Thatch envisioned and Hank now imagined. He could have no inkling of the magnitude of the life-altering situation that was about to be thrust upon him and the others.

Chapter 8

The bombing of the Ho Chi Minh trail by the Americans steadily progressed southward. The mayhem moved methodically as it pockmarked its way closer to the main trail's intersection with the east-west trail leading to Hong Tre.

The North Vietnamese foot traffic heading south was extremely heavy. Something big was obviously in the planning stages, and the Americans were determined to not only disrupt the southward flow of the enemy but also to rain total hell down on them. This hour would bring the most intense local bombing of the Ho Chi Minh trail in the history of the Vietnam War. Many people would die on this dreadful day.

The winding main trail was covered by triple foliage in most but not all of the local area. The bombs were dropped from B-52s in a blanketing pattern in hopes of some direct hits. The outcome of this carpet bombing was always left to conjecture by others. Craters marked the landscape everywhere. When there was an occasional direct hit on the trail, the overflow earth from the surrounding craters was used by the travelers to repair the damage while the ebb and flow of life on the trail continued.

Nevertheless, the bombs didn't have to hit the pathway directly to cause havoc. The shock and awe of the massive explosions drove many combatants to total despair and completely destroyed their will to continue on their paths. Additionally, compounding the air assault on the trail were the C-130 flying gunships, which were basically cargo airplanes converted into flying gun platforms. They were known in American jargon as Spookies or Puff the Magic Dragon.

The mystical names for these flying agents of death were well-deserved. The door-mounted, electronically controlled Gatling guns would train a tracer-illuminated stream of hi-powered projectile fire downward in a death ray. This concentration of firepower inflicted untold carnage. It was later believed that this weapon of war caused more damage and death on the Ho Chi Minh trail than all the bombing from the B-52s.

This day's early morning aerial activity was one of the finest hours for the C-130s. They followed in rotation after the bombers left the air space and hit the trail where the foliage was the thinnest. Electronically, the crew had the ability to track movement in the dark, and this particular early dawn they hit pay dirt. There were thousands of foot soldiers on the move along the trail. The troops were strung out in large groups stretching thousands of yards with little or no spacing in between them for safety.

They caught one such group of northern regulars with their pants down. The crew of a C-130 observed and tracked their movement through the thinner foliage. When the command to fire was executed from afar, those in the crew's sights were literally raked to pieces by the death ray. The carnage was god-awful, and the results were cheered from above. It was all in a good day's work.

The trail below was massive chaos. Troops scattered in self–preservation, and as they paused to lift a fallen comrade, the grasped arm or leg of a wounded comrade would just separate from the body. Out of the twelve hundred or so enemy souls on that particular section on the trail, only fifty survived the compounded onslaught. The others were shredded into scattered body parts. Of the fifty survivors, some of whom were seriously wounded, a group of twenty-nine sought refuge to the west, along the trail leading to Hong Tre.

Their survival plan was to get as far away from the trail before daybreak to avoid the next round of aerial attacks that was sure to follow. Thus, they trekked farther into Laos, seeking respite and safety. As they moved westward along the trail, they felt a diehard air of confidence that they would live to fight another day. They hustled along in disciplined unison with a veteran non-officer now in charge. They were hidden by a welcome canopy of jungle overgrowth. He ordered them to follow along until, in his judgment, they were a safe distance from the sure-to-return enemy bombardment.

At the appropriate time, and only then, they would rest. He and only he would decide when it was safe to resume their southward journey back on the trail. There was not a word of dissent. Then fate intervened. The lead man stepped on one of Hank's well-placed land mines. It blew him practically in half. The others froze in panic. The self-appointed leader rushed forward, telling them to stay on the path and not to rush into the cover of the bush.

He had immediately realized no hail of gunfire followed the explosion and therefore it was not an ambush. This guy knew his stuff and ordered them to continue on the path, hoping it had been just a random mine. But then the second mine blew another man apart, and they were quickly reduced in number from twenty-nine down to twenty-seven. Their leader now thought otherwise of his previous decision and ordered them all to immediately abandon the trail. They would now move slowly through the bush. These additional losses fueled their anger, and they were now thirsty for blood. Someone nearby had to have placed those mines.

The rooftops of the stilted huts in Hong Tre suddenly came into view. There they were, right in front of them—a series of huts in a clear wide-open field. What wonderful targets of opportunity they would become. This haggard group of survivors would now have their revenge, and they all knew the drill. First would come the killing, then the plunder. It was instinctive and matter-of-fact after all these years of war.

****

The previously gathered group of four, now huddled at the bunker, heard the first mine blow. They instinctively took a knee to lower their profile. They looked to Hank.

"Shit. Someone is on the trail. Quickly arm yourselves. Hayrack, you set up the machine gun. Don't let them reach the settlement. You others take up a weapon. Everyone know how to use an AK?"

Thatch answered in the negative but quickly retorted, "But I'm deadly with a sidearm."

Hank responded. "Here, take these RPGs in the canvas carriers. Grasp as many of these fuckers as you can carry. Remember, quantity saves the day. Load up and stay with me, and here, take this .45, but I want it back."

Jim, now caught up in Hank's frantic pace, grabbed an AK-47 and loaded a magazine. He had some quick questions about chambering a round and removing the safety, but they were quickly resolved. Jim stuffed extra loaded magazines everywhere but up his ass and spread out along the tree line. He took a position twenty to thirty yards to the west, carrying two AK-47s and a mule load of ammo. Hank spread an equal distance to the east with his AK-47. Thatch humped two RPG launchers and at least ten projectiles and positioned himself with Hank. Hayrack stayed at the bunker with the machine gun. They were unlocked, loaded, and lying in wait for unknown intruders.

The now heavily armed group of four hoped that whoever was approaching the settlement from the east was already dead from the land mines. Nevertheless, if they survived the mines, they had better be friendly looking or all hell would greet them as they exited the safety of the wooded cover. If they ventured into the open field with any observable hostile intent, all bets would be off.

The defensive four, now positioned with their wits gathered about them, divided their concern between the perceived enemy approaching on the trail and the others in the settlement, who had hurried indoors upon hearing the mines explode. Additionally, the four men had completely forgotten about the return of the invited guests that were due from the west end of the settlement.

No matter! It hit the fan so fast, it just didn't matter. The first enemy RPG onslaught began out of the east tree line where the east-west trail transitioned from wooded area to the clearing of the field. The huts were immediately and systematically leveled. There were several RPG shooters, and the poor souls in the huts were wiped out in the ensuing inferno. The women, children, and old men died where they cowered in each other's arms, hiding from the evil spirits.

Immediately following the devastating RPG attack, a strategically separated group of twelve combatants moved out of the trees and into the field leading into Hong Tre. Hayrack was just about to open fire on them with the machine gun when the balance of the enemy force opened fire upon him from the rear. The attackers had spotted the men's telltale movement earlier along the tree line and had sent fifteen of their men in a circuitous route to outflank them and move in directly behind them. The multiple attacks were well-timed and equally well-executed. Hank and his boys were now caught in a potentially deadly cross fire.

Hayrack took off some pressure when he opened up on the twelve that were about one hundred yards in front of his position. His fire killed or pinned most of them to the ground among the rubble of the destroyed huts. Four of twelve, however, passed directly through the settlement and took up a defensive position just out of sight at the far western end of the settlement.

The fifteen men positioned behind the surrounded group of four fired at will and closed fast toward them. The trees provided cover, but they also hindered the effectiveness of their fire. Thatch launched as many RPG rounds toward them as he possibly could. It was no matter, for they would soon overrun the outnumbered few as planned.

Hank was decisive. He grabbed Thatch by the arm and moved recklessly toward Hayrack and the machine gun position. "Pour it on those bastards in the settlement. Keep them pinned. We're going to attack toward them. Follow fast when you can once we take the upper hand."

Hayrack knew his position. Those behind him would soon be upon him. This would be his last stand. *"Adieu, bon chance, bon ami,"* he called.

Hank responded emotionally with a firm nod of his head and quickly motioned to the other two to follow him onto the path, retracing their steps past the planted mines toward the settlement and the waiting enemy.

While Hayrack pinned the attackers down with withering machine gun fire, Hank's advance was successful. By the time Hayrack's fire abruptly stopped, Jim and Hank started theirs and effectively dispatched the five or six men Hayrack hadn't killed.

The fifteen attackers in the jungle quickly overran Hayrack, who had run out of ammunition. He continued to return fire with an AK-47 until they killed him. Buoyed with confidence, the attackers—now numbering ten—charged toward the three survivors in the still-burning settlement. The frenzy of their charge carried them directly into the mine field. Silhouetted by the flames, they became grotesque targets as they were individually blown apart. Some died with their initial first step into the open field. A few turned to retreat, only to find a mine underfoot. Some charged forward, seeming to know their fate and wanting to be in charge until the bitter end. Several survived by freezing in their tracks and raising their arms skyward in surrender.

They were immediately fired upon by Jim and Hank, and as they fell to the ground, the impact of their bodies set off two more mines. A fitting end seemed to be acknowledged in the ensuing eye contact of the two shooters. Then all three immediately looked toward Attapeu. They checked their weapons, reloaded, and went on the move.

The four surviving attackers positioned to the near west were next in their sights. Hank, Jim, and Thatch had tasted blood, and they wanted more. The vision of the huts and their inhabitants blown to smithereens fueled their rage. They wanted it finished to the very last man.

Hank motioned for them to spread out. Then he cautiously moved forward with Jim to his right and Thatch to his left. A slight knoll stood between them and the perceived enemy position. They were totally unprepared for what they saw as they crawled to the edge of the knoll and took a cautious peek.

Chapter 9

Previously, while Hank, Jim, Thatch, and Hayrack had moved from Hank's hut to the weapons bunker, the rolling thunder of the bombing on the trail had obscured another background sound that was familiar to some but under different circumstances would have been heard by all.

An unmarked Huey had come in at treetop level and landed just west of Hong Tre. The pilot landed at the edge of the field near the western tree line. The unarmed Huey sat about five hundred yards out of sight from the settlement, with the engine running at idle and the rotors still turning slowly. Out stepped the recently christened sunshine boys.

The boys and their pilot had flown in from nearby Attapeu earlier than expected. While their pilot stayed with the Huey, the two strangers started walking on the path toward the knoll, which obscured their view of the settlement. They both commented on the intensity of the distant sound of the bombing activity on the north-south trail.

When the first barrage of the enemy RPGs hit into the settlement huts, they both abruptly hit the deck. They froze on the ground, motionless in awe of the unexpected sound of the brief but fatal attack on the huts. Not knowing what was happening, they both assumed some wayward munitions from the trail bombing had been dropped on the settlement. They crept forward to assess their position; both were determined not to leave without Thatcher Pittsford in tow.

They slowly advanced into the onrushing arms of four North Vietnamese regular army soldiers that came charging over the knoll. The soldiers had intended to position themselves along the tree line in a defensive position, but the Huey now occupied that space.

The four soldiers so surprised the boys that they had no time to react other than to raise their arms. The four aggressors motioned with their weapons for the two to turn toward the tree line and start walking.

At the very same moment, the Huey pilot observed the situation and attempted to throttle up his Huey as the group approached him. Two of the four soldiers shot several times through the Plexiglas. The pilot was killed instantly; his twisted grip on the collective control released, and the chopper returned to its idle.

The sunshine boys were now totally cognizant of the hopelessness of their position. They were armed with pistols but totally out-gunned. Their now useless automatic rifles were still aboard the Huey. Their pilot was dead, and the enemy was now upon them, removing their concealed pistols. It couldn't have gotten much worse for them.

While two of the captors bound their prisoners' hands behind their backs, the other two smiled, one of whom was the senior non-officer leader that had planned the attack on the settlement. He was feeling his oats, and while keeping his AK-47 leveled on his captives, he motioned with his head over toward the settlement. He flashed a broad smile.

Obviously, the incursion was going well. The four all nodded and smiled toothy grins as the sounds of the fight faded. Had it not been for these two captives, they would have enjoyed watching the turkey shoot from the edge of the grassy knoll. However, these two obviously important individuals, one surely an American, were prime captives. All of the soldiers' thoughts focused on how best to capitalize on this magnificent happening.

That's when the first of two RPG rounds landed about fifty feet from them with an accompanying loud explosion. The soldiers looked around in disbelief that their troops would have fired in their direction. Thatch's ruse successfully distracted them.

The two captives helplessly fell prone to the ground. Then the first of three shots rang out. The first was a head shot that dropped the first of the formerly smiling duo. Hank had practiced over the years with the AK-47 and had just proven himself a damn good shot.

At the same time Hank's shot hit its target, two additional rapid-fire shots rang out and hit the remaining smiler—the leader of the pack—in the chest. Jim had no practice with the AK-47, but he was a good shot in his own right. However, he played it safe with multiple body shots rather than a single head shot. This was his first up-close-and personal kill; the others in the settlement had been rapid-fire spray shots aimed at multiple scrambling individuals. However, the others that he had killed in the past from the air with his Huey had been erased from his mind.

Without hesitation or the need to reload, Hank and Jim repeated with three more shots, and then all four of the former enemies lay dead on the ground at the feet of the shaking and now standing CIA twosome, who had stood as a result of the impulse to run into the bush before they themselves became the next targets in this shooting gallery.

Jim called out and immediately put some wind back into their sails. "Hey, you two okay?"

They remained motionless but cautiously turned their heads and looked toward the approaching pack. It was then that they observed two armed individuals with their weapons at their sides walking toward them and a third person indirectly behind them. The sun was rising behind the approaching three, and though the two men were unable to shade their eyes because they lacked a free hand, they stood tall and cautiously squinted as best they could.

The scene would have been hilarious to Hank and Jim under other circumstances, but as they approached the two hand-bound individuals, their minds were on different tracks. Thatch was also weighing his options. He caressed the .45 with his left hand while firmly holding the pistol in his right. Although the safety was off, he had not fired a round and thus possessed a full magazine. He was an excellent shot with targets, and there were only four stationary people in front of him: Hank, Jim, and the two bounty hunters who had been on his trail. Possibly it was time for a clean break. His mind ran in circles, fueled by adrenaline.

Jim thought it was prudent for cooler heads to prevail. He felt there would be plenty of time later for grieving, but at the same time, he mentally acknowledged to himself that he had very little to grieve about. Neither was it the right time for any impulsive moves or rash decisions on anyone's part. Jim took a quick inventory of everyone's body language. It was a sight to behold.

Hank was weighing the option of shooting Thatch in front of the CIA guys, thus depriving them of their target. Then he thought that if he was going to do that, he might as well shoot the two CIA guys. *What the hell?* he thought. *There's no Hong Tre for anyone to come back to destroy.* His spirit broke slightly with that thought, for he realized there was nothing left for him there either. After twelve years, there was absolutely nothing. He remained tense and unusually silent.

Thatch looked at the two CIA guys standing before him, looking so damn helpless. He saw them for just what they were in his mind—a couple of educated mercenaries. He looked at Jim and Hank and then back to the two exhausted bloodhounds. Neither appeared to have much hunt left in him.

His thoughts continued. Life on the run sucked, and he was tired of it. He had lost all interest in the Good Book. He thought if he had put as much energy into his own life as he had into the lives of others, things somehow would have been different. Then Thatch suddenly had an epiphany. He would go back only if Hank and Jim would agree to accompany him. He would not leave them behind for the CIA to come back and eliminate.

All of his thinking was not very clear, and his mind started to wander. He began to realize that he actually knew very little about the damn CIA. Without any warning, he steadily began to run out of adrenaline, and his thought processes proceeded to shut down. Meanwhile, Jim walked over to the strangers with a smile. He turned the tall American away from him and stepped up behind him. The shorter fellow, standing within the shadow of the two, observed Jim nervously as he had produced a bayonet he had removed from Hank's supply bunker.

"What's your name?" Jim asked and patiently waited for an answer.

None was forthcoming.

Luther "Luke" Klackston was a college-educated former jock that had joined the CIA after an army career that had spanned ten years, from 1946 to 1956. He had served in Korea with distinction in army intelligence. He had joined the CIA in order to stay involved in the intelligence field but to be free of the constraints imposed by the military code of conduct. He was a perfect agent. He loved the freedom that operating in Southeast Asia offered, and he guarded the fringe benefits of that freedom as if they were the Holy Grail. There was no way he was going to give his name to some son-of-a-bitch that was intending to slit his throat.

"Listen, you stubborn prick, if you want your hands cut free, the least you can do is tell me your goddamn name," Jim said.

Luke breathed a sigh of relief. *Maybe I'm reading a bit too much into this situation,* he thought. "Luke. My name is Luke, Luke Klackston."

With that, Jim cut his bindings and stepped around in front of him. As Luke rubbed his wrists, Jim handed him the bayonet and safely backed away. "My name is Jim. Here, cut your buddy loose." As he stepped away from Hank, he turned toward the other man. "What's your name?"

With no hesitation, Anthony Toynache responded, "Tony, Tony Toynache. And before you ask, my mother was Italian."

With that, the air lightened a bit. However, the ensuing silence suggested that whoever spoke up next would lose. There was still some fight in them all, but the enemy had yet to be determined. Jim decided to break the stalemate. He quickly removed the banana magazine from his AK-47 and looked at it as if to count the remaining rounds. He threw it to the ground, inserted a new fully loaded magazine, and proceeded to chamber a round. The AK-47 was ready for more action, and it now sat on Jim's hip. His message of impatience was not lost on any of the others.

Luke spoke up. "Thatch, you know we have to do our best to return you to Udorn. Don't take it personally. It's just our assignment. Quite frankly, we really do not know why you are wanted back there. The boss just told us to find you and return you. However, we now find ourselves at your mercy. We can turn our backs, but you know full well that without proof of your death, others will come looking for you. It is completely out of our control. You know where we stand in the pecking order. Do you have any suggestions to move this situation off dead center?"

Tony nodded in agreement.

Thatcher responded, "Look guys. I panicked and skipped because I just didn't want that life anymore. Now standing here and weighing all options, it wasn't so bad. I'll go back if you will make allowances for my friends to come back with me." Thatch thought of the carnage just over the knoll behind them. He thought of Hank and his family and the others.

Tony now spoke up, "Fellows, we don't give a big rat's ass who goes where as long as Thatch goes back to where he came from. However, there is one catch. Right now I don't know how in the hell any of us are going to get from here to there."

Luke continued, "We have a landing strip quite a distance from here in an area that is controlled by people that are friendly to us. A plane from Air America will meet us there this afternoon and fly us to Udorn. From there, everyone except Thatch can go his own way."

Tony then interjected, "There's one big catch though. Unfortunately, we cannot travel over land between here and the airfield without losing our hides to the unfriendly factions that control the surrounding area. That's why we came in by air, and that's why we need to get out by air. Otherwise, we are screwed. To compound matters, we are also out of radio contact range as long as we are on the ground."

Hank saw the merit in what Tony said and began to think that this was indeed the time to get out of this part of Laos. He knew Jim could fly the damn Huey, but he just knew Jim couldn't get there. Mentally, he wasn't capable. At least that is what he thought.

While all the jawing was taking place, Jim had walked over to the Huey to check out the dead pilot. He removed him from the cockpit and placed him as gently as he could in the back of the chopper. He seemed to be operating by rote. The dead go in the back. The dead go in the back.

Then Jim did something unexpected. He strapped himself into the now empty right seat and brought up the power. The engine whined louder and louder, and the rotor gained more and more speed. He unconsciously scanned the engine gauges and the rest of the cockpit. He observed holes in the side window where the deadly projectiles had entered and struck the dead pilot. He winced as he stared at several projectile exit holes in the radio and navigation equipment.

Jim shook his head and thought, *Screwed again.*

The grounded four looked at each other in obvious disbelief. They immediately began a head low, hunching beeline through the knee-high grass toward the open side door of the Huey. Jim motioned with one raised finger for Hank to sit in the left seat opposite him. Hank complied. The remaining three, along with the former pilot, filled up the rear.

Jim turned to Hank as he waited for the gauges to indicate he had enough power for lift off. "Anything more you want to tell me about my past?"

The noise would have canceled out anything Hank would have proffered. However, Hank offered nothing except a long stare out the side window. He knew he would have to have some answers on the other end, wherever that might be. Following Jim's lead, he turned and placed a nearby hanging set of earphones on his head and returned to his vacant outboard staring.

All aboard except Jim were startled by their first stop. Jim landed smack dab in the middle of the destroyed settlement for some unfinished business. It also gave him some much-needed practice at the controls so he could determine if he could indeed actually fly the beast.

They looked for survivors and found none. They found Hayrack with three dead bodies around him. They proceeded to bury only their own. The CIA guys more than carried their weight with the burials. They were extremely sensitive to the mood of the survivors and had obviously experienced battlefield deaths in the past. After finishing the gruesome task, they quickly headed back to the Huey and were buckling in when Luke leaned forward and lifted Jim's headset. "Set a course due west, and we'll adjust as we go. We need to fly into Thailand. By the way, we usually fly at least three thousand feet above ground level. RPGs and stuff like that, you know."

Jim turned toward Luke and responded in a captain like mode, "We have no navigation equipment other than the sun at our backs. This ride will be what is known as dead reckoning, my friend. So pick out any landmarks you remember from your outbound ride, and keep me informed."

Jim left him with a head nod and a wry smile. He was enjoying the rush and not knowing what was waiting for him on the other end. He decided to enjoy the moment. He had no idea what was in the cards for him or the others, and he didn't care. He gave Hong Tre a solemn backward glance as they lifted off.

The day had been traumatic for Jim. He had experienced war up close and personal, and it did not sit well with him. As they flew along at an unknown altitude, he thought of all the carnage he had observed in the settlement and how few bodies they had been able to find whole and bury. They had filled one mass grave with as many body parts as possible.

Jim also attempted to undertake a self-examination of what was occurring as he deftly flew the Huey westward. How in the hell did he know how to fly such a beast? There he sat with a powerful helicopter tightly strapped on his back, and it felt so damn comfortable. It was as though the craft was part of him and he were a part of it.

He mentally backtracked, with bobble headed nods, but he could only go back as far as the night of his collapse and subsequent blackout on the trail leading into Hong Tre. That was where his memory stopped dead in its tracks. *One hell of a deal* was all he could mouth as he shook his head as if to clear it. He knew he needed to concentrate on the situation at hand.

At takeoff, the fuel gauges had indicated half-full. Jim wondered if it required half of the onboard fuel to reach Hong Tre from the airstrip in Thailand. He mentally noted that on the return trip, they were now flying into the wind, which would considerably shorten their flying range.

Unaware of the potential fuel shortage situation, everyone else on board had settled in for the long ride. As a final merciful gesture for his passengers, before departing Hong Tre, Jim— along with ready assistance from Hank—had removed the dead pilot's body from the rear of the craft and carefully placed him in the co-pilot seat. Hank was elated to be out of the hot seat next to Jim. It took some soul-searching by all aboard to get used to the dead pilot's body up front. Nevertheless, the passengers in the rear were grateful not to be sharing the ride with the dead man.

"This should be an interesting trip," Jim said aloud to his copilot.

Obviously, no response was forthcoming, and none was expected. This would be Brian's last ride up front. He deserved the dignity.

Hank sat quietly as his mentally and physically exhausted body absorbed the engine noise and the sound of the rotating blades. Both combined to create in him an inner beat that timed itself to his churning, overactive mind. His family was gone, and his heart ached. His home was gone, and for the first time in a long time, he feared the future.

He had never been aloft in any type of aircraft, and he was actually scared. Intertwined tightly but volcano like with his anguish was a well-primed mental time bomb of hot molten anger. Hank basically was pissed off at life in general, and as an uncontrollable rage began to roil within him, he would soon shift from one set of emotions to another and begin to plan his revenge. The recipients of said revenge had yet to be determined.

Tony and Luke were relieved. Although neither of them had ever experienced anything like the aftermath at Hong Tre, they had seen death up close and personal as early military advisers in Vietnam. Since resigning from the military and joining the CIA, they had anticipated a return to their military role in Laos. They were both relieved to have an end in sight for their current assignment. Their eyes met several times, and they mentally expressed the same thought: they would gladly throw Thatch Pittsford out of the damn craft if either of them thought they could get away with it. He had caused them much pain and delay from their anticipated CIA adviser assignments.

Thatcher Pittsford was regaining his wits and internalizing the various options that may be awaiting him in northern Laos. He was sure the CIA station chief, whomever he now might be, and the colonel would be standing by for him once word reached them that he had been found and was en route to Udorn. Nevertheless, for now he had some quality time to think about how he would present his financial acumen to the tainted powers-at-be and deftly carve out a piece of the money pie for himself. Thatch had completely given up on the Bible. He had seen hell in Hong Tre, and he had survived it in good order. The old Wall Street guy was mentally returning to his roots, and today they ran deep.

It wasn't too long, possibly less than an hour, before a long river appeared on the horizon. Running north to south, Luke identified it with an excited arm stretched gesture that brought some relief to the pent-up anxiety onboard.

"That's the Mekong River up ahead, and that big bend in the river is a very welcome landmark!" he exclaimed.

"The Fence," as the Mekong was oftentimes called by pilots operating out of Thailand, was the border between Laos and Thailand.

Luke continued, "I'll watch for some telltale local landmarks, and we should be home free. We need to fly to the river, and then I'm pretty sure we need to turn north up the river for about ten or so miles to find the airstrip."

Jim asked a pointed question, "Luke, ballpark it. About how long until we reach the airfield?"

"Thirty minutes, max."

"Luke, we have no more than fifteen to twenty minutes of fuel left onboard. You all can jump out now and lighten the load, or we need to find the field pronto. If you are sure that the field is north, then I'm heading northwest right now. Keep an eye peeled."

All conversation onboard ceased.

Chapter 10

The country of Laos had been somewhat of an enigma throughout most of its history. Ruled alternately by kings and powerful families down through the centuries, it had been under the widespread colonial thumbprint of the French since the 1800s. Toward the end of the French influence and with the beginning of the American war in Vietnam, Laos had been engaged in turmoil once again.

In 1968, three distinct factions jockeyed for position and power. One faction was communist inspired and supported by their neighbor and long-time antagonist, North Vietnam. Another homegrown faction sought neutrality at all costs and a third faction, though tired of the exiting French influence, aligned with the United States.

This third faction was in power under the American influence and was basically a figurehead. Backed with massive covert military support from the United States and additional manpower support from neighboring Thailand, this combined faction was a formidable force. Thus ensued a guerilla war with the homegrown, North-Vietnam-supported revolutionary Pathet Lao and an all-out conflict with the invading North Vietnamese regular army. Most, if not all, of the conflict was centered in northern Laos in an area known as the Plain of Jars.

The communist factions grew out of the despair of many Laotians, who grew to distrust not only the French but also the puppet leadership historically comprised of members from twenty-five powerful Laotian families that collectively controlled their country. Their control was absolute.

The capital of Laos, Vientiane, was located in the west central portion of Laos, and the entire north central portion of the country was in conflict.

The southern portion was comparatively quiet. However, many peasants from the south—though not communists—traveled to the north to join the Pathet Lao in their struggle for independence. They were just tired of the French influence in their lives.

North Vietnam had always had a close eye on its western neighbor. With their war in the south with America growing in intensity every day, the North Vietnamese needed to protect their supply route to the south, which was the Ho Chi Minh trail.

Contrary to the understanding of many civilian Americans, the Ho Chi Minh trail ran the length of eastern Laos and was not in Vietnam itself. Therefore, the North Vietnamese invaded the eastern portion of Laos to protect their supply line. They also supplied and supported the Pathet Lao.

Aligned against this duo was a combination of Hmong tribesmen, Laotian military, and Thailand conscripts. Their leaders were figuratively Laotian army officers, but in reality they were led by former American military men now working for the CIA. On the record, there were no American military personnel in Laos. Off the record, the former American military men—now in the employ of the CIA—were doing a terrific job in blunting the advances of the enemy. They didn't win every military encounter, but they made their presence known and won much more than their figurative fair share.

Basically, what the American Green Berets did with the Montinguard tribesmen in the early years of the Vietnam War, these CIA advisors were doing with the Hmong tribesmen. Additionally, they also organized, trained, and commanded the green fighting men sent in from Thailand.

The enemy controlled the eastern sectors of the country, and the CIA army controlled the west. Together they fought over everything in between. This vast plain area of Laos surrounded by mountains was collectively known as Plain de Jars or the Plain of Jars. The entire plateau was so named due to the scattered presence of hundreds of large jars that were carved out of granite. These jars measured three to ten feet tall and dated back twenty-five hundred years. Their intended use had never been determined.

The entire American operation required untold tons of subsidence and military supplies. The Hmong lived in the eastern mountains, and their CIA advisors lived among them. The other CIA-led forces moved to where the action was, fought to resolution, and then were redirected elsewhere to fight another day. The logistics were a monumental undertaking considering there were supposedly no Americans in Laos.

Enter another CIA-backed and covertly financed solution—Air America. Air America was a covert airline like no other in the world. However, it had some similarities to the former American Civil Air Transport (CAT) program that supported the Chinese nationalists on mainland China prior to their demise.

Air America, though terribly maligned by the subsequent conspiracy theory mentality that in later years infected rational thought in the States, performed the herculean task of ferrying men and supplies into and out of various remote and perfidious locations in Laos. Though the various fixed-wing airplanes and helicopters were unarmed, many times they flew into areas of extreme danger to deliver or retrieve people and supplies.

Unknown by many Americans even in present-day was the fact that Air American pilots, while on routine flight duty, would divert from their assigned destinations to risk life and limb to rescue American airman that had been shot down over Laos. The beeping of a locator beacon was received by a cockpit radio, and it would draw immediate response from any nearby Air America pilot. These pilots knew that if the downed pilot wasn't rescued within twenty to thirty minutes, he would be found by enemy ground forces and taken prisoner or killed on the spot. A similar fate was met by more than a few of the Air America pilots.

Conversely, the U.S. Air Force had rescue helicopters, affably referred to as jolly green giants, on standby at airfields in Thailand for rescue operations. However, these rescue craft and their well-trained crews, were many times unable to reach a downed airman within the life-or-death capture window of twenty to thirty minutes.

It has been said that untold numbers of Air America pilots would have received some of the highest military honors as a result of their daring rescue diversions if they had been part of the active military rather than civilian pilots.

Laos was a surreal, land-locked country in Southeast Asia that bordered on the mystical land of Siam (Cambodia). This secretive, politically diverse, combative, and supposedly non-American military occupied piece of ancient real estate was the exact place where destiny was preparing to eventually hand-deliver and unceremoniously dump Jim McDonnell, Hank Lamont, and Thatch Pittsford. However, they would make some life-altering intermediate stops along the way that would better prepare them to meet the challenges that would follow in Laos.

Chapter 11

The approach and landing at the obscure, short, and dusty airstrip was uneventful. The strip had come into view just as Luke had predicted. There had been no radio contact due to the onboard collateral damage that had resulted from some errant AK-47 fire earlier at Hong Tre.

Nonetheless, they were safely on the ground in Thailand. As Jim instinctively watched the gauges and waited for the engine to cool before he shut it down, the machine quit. The damn thing had just run completely out of fuel.

The five of them sat there with their heads down in disbelief. Was this a harbinger of things to come? Not one word was spoken as they disembarked and walked toward a ramshackle shack with an armed individual sitting beside it. He was perched on an olive green fifty-gallon drum and had an older American M-14 weapon on his lap and a lighted hand-rolled cigarette dangling from his mouth. The ashes dropped onto his weapon as he spoke in heavily accented English.

"Been expecting you two, but where's Brian, and who are these three?"

"Brian's dead. He's still strapped in the crate." Tony pointed over his shoulder with his thumb in the direction of the now-silent Huey.

"And these three?"

Tony continued with a brief direct response. "They're with us. Jim here is now our pilot. No more questions, only answers."

There were no introductions, and the question man now became the answer man.

"What's the scoop on our ride?" Luke seemed to grow impatient.

"Your ride is on its way. I just heard from him, and he should be wheels down any time now.

Tony took the local watchdog aside and instructed him to arrange a ride for Brian back to Bangkok. The man informed Tony that he knew the routine and would take care of everything.

Luke spoke up again. "Can our ride handle the extra passengers?"

"No sweat. It's a Volpar."

A Volpar was an older Beechcraft twin-engine plane. Once a favorite of American oil companies, the B-18 had been converted and modernized. The rear tail landing gear had been replaced by an under-nose mounted wheel that changed the landing gear configuration to what is known as a tricycle gear. The plane no longer sat nose high and now landed in a conventional flare. The old oil-gulping radial engines had been replaced by more powerful turbine engines. It was indicative of the familiar saying that one could not overload the beast.

So far, this dismal torrid day really sucked. The emotional tide of the morning massacre at Hong Tre and the gut-wrenching aftermath had left all five travelers physically and mentally exhausted. After the rather rough Huey ride, the comfort of the Volpar did not go unnoticed. The ride was smooth; the mood was lighter but still silent. All aboard the aircraft were astonished by the amount of air traffic they observed in spite of the fact that Udorn was nowhere in sight.

By habit, Jim had elected to sit up front with the pilot, who was a former marine aviator by the name of Louie, who had resigned from the Corps to sign on with Air America. Without knowing Jim's background other than he had flown the Huey in place of Brian, Louie accepted him as a fellow aviator. Louie had known Brian and queried Jim about his demise. Jim deflected his question by telling him he was not authorized to talk about the mission.

The response piqued Louie's interest, and he continued his questioning, "So, you're with the agency, not Air America?"

"No, I didn't say that," Jim said.

"Well, come on. One pilot to another, what the hell happened to Brian?" Louie was not going to let go of the subject.

"Wrong place at the wrong time. That's it," Jim responded with finality, and Louie tactfully let it go.

"So, you're not CIA and not Air America?"

"That's right, Louie. I'm just freelancing right now," Jim said.

"How's the pay?"

Jim laughed for the first time in a long, long time. "The pay, Louie? The pay is god-awful. I can't remember the last time I was this broke."

"Hmmm," Louie responded while scanning his gauges and glancing outside the plane as if to look for landmarks. They flew on in silence both in the front of the plane and the rear. The passengers in the rear were either asleep or nodding off.

The silence, broken only by the whine of the Volpar's engines, seemed to bother Louie because he once again nonchalantly struck up some seemingly idle conversation after first contacting Udorn air traffic control.

"So, what do you fly, Jim?"

God, Jim thought, *this guy is going to drive me crazy with his questions.* His mind began to search for something to say. He was almost at a loss to answer the damn question but he responded, "Lately, Louie, mostly Hueys."

"Any fixed wing?"

"Not for some time." It was the best response Jim could muster, and he needed to get off of the subject fast. "Tell me, Louie, why do you ask?"

"Would you like to make some money flying?" Louie's answer came back fast. It was direct and to the point.

"Money? Make money flying what and where?"

Louie had Jim's attention, and now Jim had Louie talking instead of asking questions. Jim relaxed a little and listened. Louie obviously spent too much time alone in the cockpit, and when presented with a captive audience, he was prone to pontificate.

"Well, Jim, Air America is really ramping up after a year or so of cutbacks. Something big must be on the horizon because we have all been offered recruiting bonuses for any volunteers we bring into the fold." He continued, "Are you familiar with Air America?"

"Why don't you fill me in on the details?"

Louie did just that. For the remainder of the flight, Jim got an earful, and the more he heard about AA, the more interested he became.

"Keep an eye out for traffic. You can't believe how busy this damn place can be. Actually, I'm told Udorn is one of the busiest airports in the world right now."

Jim began to rubberneck as he casually asked Louie, "How does she handle on final?"

"Smooth," was the other man's one-word answer, quickly followed by, "Would you like to take her in?"

"Sure. If you're okay with that!" Jim said.

"Did you ever fly a Volpar, or did I ask you that already? Never mind. How about I set her up on final approach and you take over from there?"

"Roger that."

The others had no idea what was taking place between the two flyboys. Hank probably would have had a heart attack.

After they lined up on final approach, Louie lifted his hand from the yoke and said, "It's all yours. Set about twenty degrees of flap before reaching the threshold and hold your speed at around one hundred knots. Keep your power up until you flair. Basically, get the nose up a little and just fly her right on to the runway. Remember, keep your power up. Land her a little long so we don't have to taxi all that far. I'll handle communications with ground control. You got all that?"

"Roger that, Louie."

"The wind is right down the runway. Piece of cake."

Louie didn't say another word to Jim until they were stopped on the tarmac at the Air America side of the long, broad, hard-surfaced runway. The U.S. Air Force occupied the other side of the field, which included extensive aircraft maintenance facilities. The Royal Thai Air Force, under the command of General Yamane Korat, ostensibly ran the entire facility of Udorn.

General Korat was an extremely important player in everything that transpired on or around the base. His ties to the CIA, Air America, and a certain Laotian general known as TN were legendary.

While cutting the engines and applying the parking brakes, Louie summarized, "Let me know if you're interested in flying for us. I could use the bonus bucks. Oh! By the way, you three, leave your weapons in the plane. If you walk off this bird with a weapon in hand, you'll probably get your asses shot off."

Thatcher was the next to be heard from. "Boys, we got company waiting for us."

The interior of the plane grew quiet once again, but no one was at rest.

Chapter 12

W.B. Coade was the CIA Station Chief and he ran the secret war in Laos. Bill Coade was a no-nonsense guy that was a total stranger to spit and polish. He was a big guy with a big-barreled chest and a matching gut directly underneath. His hair was short on top and long on the neck. Prematurely gray, he looked a bit older than his thirty-eight years. He was always clean shaven and had a problem with people and their facial hair. He kept that fact to himself unless he was drinking.

His clothing wore him, and the permanent wrinkles in the material matched those under his eyes. He drank excessively, fought at the drop of a smart-ass remark or an awkward look, and didn't believe in taking any prisoners. Most everyone liked him, and those that didn't still respected him, though they did so out of self preservation and from a safe distance.

He had only one spoken rule: don't mess with Wild Bill Coade. The word *mess* was often interchangeable with the notable "F" word, and when Wild Bill became agitated, the "F" word prevailed.

He stood on the tarmac, waiting for Thatcher Pittsford to deplane so he could personally ring his neck before turning him over to the general. Although W.B. claimed to know nothing about why the general was so pissed off at Thatch, conventional wisdom dictated that Wild Bill knew everything he had to know about anything that took or was about to take place at Udorn Thai Royal Air Force Base, the local town of Udon Thani, and parts north in Laos. It was just that he kept most things to himself.

Tony and Luke were the first to hit the tarmac. They were closely followed by Thatch, Hank, and then Jim. Louie, the pilot, was the last to deplane. Louie walked right past the group and greeted W.B. by name.

"Hi, Bill. Here's your package. He's a day or so late but hopefully not too many pounds light." They enjoyed a brief guffaw and a warm, gripping handshake as Louie turned to depart.

By *package*, Louie had of course been referring to Thatch. Bill firmly grasped the pilot's outstretched arm and hand, and they shook hands a second time. Bill then patted Louie on his right shoulder and promised to join him later for a drink. Next, he turned his attention to his two retrievers. He greeted Tony and Luke in the same manner as Louie. Bill invited them inside and then turned to the remaining three.

"You boys wait here for a minute or so. I'll be right back." Bill glanced quickly at a nearby gentleman who was positioned no more than a few meters away. Bill nodded his head with his eyes downward as if to say, *make sure they are here when I return.* The look did not go unnoticed by anyone, and the three men remained transfixed in an unconsciously defensive semicircle, all the while being eyed through the mirrored aviator sunglasses of the assigned Thai security agent.

It was obvious that Bill planned to be extensively briefed before engaging in any conversation with the three amigos. The impromptu briefing lasted longer than anyone anticipated. The watchful Thai gentleman motioned for the three men to follow him to the shade of a nearby overhang, where another equally watchful security agent standing by a nearby cooler offered them the option of water or a Coke.

The three of them sat informally at a well-worn wooden picnic table and nursed their Cokes. They were in awe of the constant flow of military air traffic as it took off and landed. It was one hell of a busy place, and it was soon to become increasingly active as the intensity of the Laotian war in the north increased. Additionally, the Americans had begun bombing North Vietnam with planes from Udorn. North Vietnam was receiving a relentless pounding.

The main event and the singular reason for their presence there that day soon materialized. Thatch paled as he noticed an official military car pull up in front of the door Bill Coade had entered. Things were about to heat up at Udorn. He grew weak in his formerly folded knees. He stood and began to pace as the former colonel, now a general, briskly walked into the nondescript one-story metal building that currently housed Bill Coade, Luke Klackston, Tony Toynache, and untold others.

General TN never looked left or right. During his straight line hustle to enter the building, his darting glance toward his gathered audience was masked by his oversize aviator-style sunglasses. Thatch soon remarked on TN's arrival and subsequent disappearance behind closed doors.

"He's one tough son-of-a-bitch boys, and when TN and Wild Bill get together, only the good Lord knows what will come out of it. It could be heaven or it could be hell and right now, I'm damn sure even the Lord ain't talking. I'm sure it's going to be hell on wheels."

It was now getting late in the afternoon, and the gathered three, although still sitting in the shade, began to ripen. In addition, they were hungry from having not eaten anything since the day before. Their minds were not on food, but their stomachs had begun to growl. No one spoke, and the commotion of the air traffic had lost its luster.

Luke and Tony suddenly exited the building and approached with a surprising good-bye smile and extended hands. They silently shook hands with each of the three, said so long with their eyes, turned on a dime, walked over to the general's car, and began to cool their heels. General TN soon followed and headed directly to his waiting car. The boys got into the rear seat, and the diminutive General TN rode shotgun.

The sound of the departing car was masked by the nearby jet engine roar that had just lit up. It distracted the gathered three long enough for Wild Bill to rejoin them practically unnoticed.

"Hey there, you three! Come on in out of the rain."

They hesitantly turned and cautiously followed Bill toward his lair as directed. It was as if each was saying to the other, *"No, you go first."* They began walking three abreast when Thatch whispered, "It's my funeral. You pall bearers fall in behind me."

Jim was the first to laugh. Hank followed with a quick grinning grunt. Hank reached out from the right and put his left arm around Thatch's shoulder. Jim followed from the left with his right arm while speaking up loud enough for Bill to hear.

"Hey, musketeers! If we go down, we all go down together."

Bill turned around and took two backward steps. For the first time, he actually gave them a head-to-toe look over. Then without hesitation, he turned to face forward again, raised his right hand in a "follow me" motion, and barked out, "You warriors need a good stiff drink."

The three men did not respond other than to quicken their pace as they closed the gap between themselves and Bill. Bill, with his giant stride, was far enough ahead that he was standing and holding the door open when they finally caught up to him.

Once inside the air-conditioned building, the comfort began to diffuse their earlier concerns that they were all in some kind of deep shit. They began to think maybe it wasn't quite as deep as they had first thought and that possibly there was a pony hidden underneath all the crap.

Bill led them into his windowless office at the end of the cool, quiet corridor. The office was sparse, the furniture nondescript. The wall pictures were ancient maps, more Woolworth than collector vintage. Two phones sat on the uncluttered desk. Light classical music played from a black plastic Sony combo eight-track/radio. The mood of the group lightened in response, especially when they spotted a paper plate with several sliced sandwiches sitting on a side table.

"Help yourselves to the chow. Wash it down with whiskey or water?"

"Both," sounded Jim. "Both will be just fine for me."

Bill looked favorably toward the stranger's response and continued, "How about you Thatch? What's your poison?"

The sarcasm did not go unnoticed by Hank, who now chimed in, "If you have Scotch, I would appreciate a good stiff Scotch with some water on the side. That would really be quenching, *mon ami*."

"Okay, Frenchie, coming right up! I like your style."

Bill now impatiently waited for Thatch to respond to his kind gesture, and the man did so right on cue. "I thought the last meal was supposed to be steak cooked just the way I like it along with a glass of milk."

Bill turned with his hands on his hips and roared, "Look, asshole, I don't know what the hell you disappeared for, and I don't give a shit that you're back. TN is happy that I got you back here, and if TN is happy, then I'm happy. That's it, over and out. Got it? It's over." Wild Bill paused for dramatic effect before continuing with his next breath. "At least as far as I'm concerned, it's over. Now, as far as General TN is concerned, that is between you and the general. By the way, Thatch, at the general's request, you are to meet with him for dinner at the Paradise Hotel tomorrow night at seven sharp. He requires that you bring with you the information he is seeking. See that you comply with his request. I will be dining with your two companions at another table out of earshot. As for now, let's eat, drink, and get acquainted. And please, boys, no bullshit. I want the truth, the whole truth, and nothing but the goddamn truth."

With that said and with his in-charge position established beyond question, Wild Bill placed the sandwich plate in front of them on his desk. Then he passed the previously poured drinks, as requested, and seated himself behind his desk. He raised his full rocks glass minus the rocks.

"Rough day for you guys. Sorry for your losses. I admire your grit. Now you need to get back on the horse."

Hank was not as ready for that pronouncement as the others. He was still painfully internalizing the crushing loss of his family. His anger continued to brew.

Wild Bill Coade, not waiting for anyone to respond, drained the glass in his right hand and refilled it from the fifth of Scotch he held in his left. Bill always buried his true emotions deep down at the bottom of a Scotch bottle.

The others passed momentarily on the food and downed their drinks in unison after touching glasses. The additional burn of the forthcoming second round of Scotch was most welcomed. As for the food? Well, the food could wait a while longer, and mandatory dinner with Bill tonight would be quite late.

Chapter 13

Previously, while Jim, Hank, and Thatcher cooled their heels outside the building under the watchful eyes of their guards, the following conversation had taken place inside Wild Bill Coade's office.

"Chief, you're not going to believe this story," Luke said.

Wild Bill despised a debriefing that started on a negative note. For Christ's sake, he had just closed the door to his office, and Luke had begun blurting out lines like a school kid caught in a prank. "Stop right there, Luke. Both of you take a seat."

Tony quietly slipped into the nearest chair and avoided any eye contact. Wide-eyed , Luke was embarrassed and circled the remaining two chairs like a dog bedding down for the night before he settled himself in a silent collapse.

W.B. stood behind them for a moment before moving past them toward his makeshift bar. Without asking, he poured three healthy glasses of Scotch. With his back still to Luke and Tony, he took a long sip from his glass and neatly refilled it to the brim before turning and slowly but deliberately placing it on his desk. This apparent stall for time perplexed the two minions, for they were anxious to get on with their extraordinary recount of the day's happenings.

W.B. turned, grasped the remaining two drinks, and simultaneously handed them to the boys. "Don't throw them down just yet. Have a sip or two while we wait for General TN. I want you two guys stone-cold sober when he arrives. Then and only then will this conversation continue."

The two men turned toward each other with raised eyebrows and sipped the mandatory sip. General Tang Now, commonly known as TN but addressed as such by only a few, soon entered Bill's office without knocking. The boys stood while Bill dragged the remaining chair around behind his desk and placed it alongside his own. General TN was a real no-nonsense guy. With the cautious approval of the Laotian government and the solid backing of the CIA, he had been charged with raising an army of Hmong warriors to defend Northeastern Laos from being overrun by their unfriendly neighbors from North Vietnam.

The North Vietnamese wanted to protect the Ho Chi Minh Trail that started in Laos and ran south; therefore, they proceeded to attack into Laos far west of the trail to protect their interests. The resulting incursion led to speculation of their real intent. Were they protecting their flank or were they preparing an all out attack on Laos? The domino theory began to gain new credence.

The powers at be in Washington D.C., through the CIA, had formulated a plan to thwart this effort with the beginning of the "secret war." The general had exceeded all expectations by forming an army that had initially exceeded ten thousand men. Coupled with the aid of the CIA and Air America, this army was trained, armed to the teeth, led by CIA operatives, and constantly re-supplied by Air America with every essential they needed to wage war on the invaders.

This juggernaut developed numerous "sites" in the remote mountains surrounding the Plain of Jars. A site consisted of a short dirt airstrip, communication capabilities, crude shelters, subsistence supplies, and munitions beyond all imagination.

General TN was the eyes and ears of this essentially guerilla army. His orders were followed without question, his requests were filled without hesitation, and his demands were numerous and at times outrageous. On the other hand, the strength of his word was legendary, and he never faltered in coming to the aid of anyone who served under him. This loyalty extended to not only his countrymen but also to the Americans. That was the bright side of the man. His dark side involved Thatcher Pittsford.

The news that Thatch was inbound to Udorn was one reason the general had been hell-bent to get to Bill's office. He also had equally pressing burr under his saddle that he intended to have Bill resolve for him posthaste.

"Gentlemen, start your engines. You are about to be debriefed." After that simple intro, Bill and TN listened intently as Luke and Tony proceeded to totally impress their distinguished audience with a gut-wrenching, detailed replay of the day. Bill refilled their glasses and his own several times during the unfolding of the events that led up to the return of Thatcher Pittsford to Udorn and into the waiting arms of General TN.

Silence followed the close of their recounting. All of their glasses were empty. The general turned to Bill and nodded. He had heard enough. "Bill, would you be so kind as to keep Thatch on ice for another day?" he asked. "I don't think there is anymore run left in him. Wouldn't you agree?"

Bill looked to Luke and Tony, who both head motioned in the affirmative.

"One other thing, Bill. I need a few moments alone with you. If you two will wait by my car, I will give you a lift to the hotel. I assume you both want to get cleaned up, and besides, I would like to have a few additional words with you."

Luke and Tony looked to Bill.

"Take twenty-four hours, guys, and let's meet for dinner tomorrow night. TN, would you like to see Thatch for dinner tomorrow? If so, I'll arrange to have him presentable."

"Bill, that would be perfect. Tomorrow, seven o'clock at the Paradise. Thank you." The General admired Bill's efficiency. He fell silent and crossed his arms. There would not be another word from him until the Luke and Tony were excused.

With a quick "get out" motion toward the door with his head, Bill excused the boys. TN turned his chair toward Bill, and in doing so, his body language indicated that he was about to ask Bill to do something munificent on his behalf.

"Bill, I want you to do something on my behalf, but first let's have another drink together."

Bill accommodated him and touched his glass with the general's glass as a sign that he was ready to hear what was on TN's mind.

"I'm tired of having my Huey shot up and not having the ability to respond in kind," the general said.

"TN, I've told you a hundred times that you instruct my guys to fly too damn low in areas you should not be flying through. In fact, it's getting difficult for me to get the Air America pilots to take the assignment as your pilot. And on top of that, your insistence on flying the damn craft once you're aloft totally pisses them off."

"Save the lecture, Bill. I know, I know. However that does not change what I have come here to ask you for."

Here we go, thought Bill.

"I want a Huey gunship. I want machines guns in the door openings, I want rocket pods, and I want my own crew with a big set of balls. I want you to arrange that for me ASAP. The future of our effort depends on you getting this done for me. You know, I ask for so little and give you so much."

"TN, let me be frank. I can get you the craft outfitted just as you want, but I cannot get you an Air America crew. Washington would remove me before granting that request."

"I anticipated that objection, Bill. Not to worry. I have already spoken to General Korat, and he has assured me that he can come up with a qualified Thai pilot and crew. However, there's more."

Bill resisted the urge to shake his head. He reached back and rubbed the back of his neck with his left hand while sipping the last of the drink in his right. He felt the need to adjust the air-conditioning to a lower setting. "Let's get it all out on the table right now, TN. What else do you require?"

"I want three of your Huey helicopters and one C-130 to start my own airline. I do not want AA pilots that are American. If you can get me Thai pilots, that's fine. My needs are immediate. Don't let me down. I've already talked with General Korat, and he will provide me with hanger space farther down on your side of the field. I'll of course need the American Air Force facilities for maintenance. Bring me some information on the crafts and pilots tomorrow night after dinner at the Paradise."

The general stood, shook hands with Bill, and flashed a confident smile that was all too familiar to Bill. "Tomorrow night then." It was not a question.

Bill returned the smile with a little resonance. *Tall order,* he thought as an old saying crossed his mind. *The impossible takes a little longer.*

The general revolved out the door, and shortly the newly arrived guests rotated in. Bill watched Hank, Jim, and Thatch wolf down the sandwiches. He had another drink but did not offer another to the others.

Two were enough for them, he thought as he calculated just how he was going to proceed with an informal interrogation.

He needed to know who the two strangers were and what their true tie to Thatch consisted of. Had Thatch, indeed, shared with them the true nature of his semi-aborted assignment from TN? If so, how was Bill to deal with that? He hated all thoughts of the damn dope thing that was going on with TN. Yet it was none of his business. His business was war, and TN was his war machine.

"Men, that's it for now. We are all going over to the Paradise Hotel and take a break. You can clean up, and I will arrange for new clothing for each of you. Then I am going to talk with each of you individually. Once that is finished, you can all go your own way, except of course Thatch. Thatch, your place is with General TN. Are we clear on that?"

"Yes, Bill."

Bill turned his attention to the other two. "After we talk, you two can hang around as my guests for a couple of days and just catch your breath. Luke and Tony will look after you. They can arrange for anything you want, within reason. I can arrange a hop into Bangkok when you're ready."

Hank and Jim looked wide-eyed at each other. Jim spoke first, "Do you prefer to be called W.B. or Bill?"

"Bill is fine."

"Okay, Bill. There's no question we need some cleaning up. However, I've got to tell you, we really do need to talk! Hank and I need some big time help with—"

Bill abruptly interrupted him. "Gentlemen! That is just what I do here. I make things happen. Shoot straight with me, and let the chips fall where they may. You have no idea what can be accomplished here at Udorn or, for that matter, anywhere else in the world."

"Bill, we will just have to take you at your word." Hank's response seemed a little desperate, but his voice was strong.

Bill picked up a phone and quickly arranged a ride for them all to proceed, indirectly, to the Paradise.

Chapter 14

In late spring of 1968, the buds on many of the trees were in full bloom, and the French lilacs in the McDonnell family's backyard were once again poised to introduce their glorious purple flowers. However, the tall landmark chestnut tree that dominated the McDonnell backyard and could be seen all the way down the back alley to the church would be without its white flowers this year. A phantom blight had killed off a random number of the area's chestnut trees. This foreboding sign was to be repeated up and down the line in the Lackawanna Valley. In the same vein of blight, the Vietnam War—over nine thousand miles away and out of sight except for television—had begun to cull some of the finest young men and women serving there, some of whom had roots still grounded back home in Scranton, Pennsylvania.

Mom McDonnell sat at the dining room table, addressing an envelope that was destined to pass through San Francisco on its way to South Vietnam. She half gathered herself, without finishing the task at hand, and responded to a firm double rap at the front door. With a little wonderment due to the late hour (nine o'clock was late to her), she greeted them silently with a gracious nod and a warm smile that immediately faded in fright as the senior of two uniformed marines proceeded to address her, "Mrs. McDonnell?"

That was all that she heard. The night air suddenly stilled. The homes across the hilly street stood at attention as if they were listening in the dark while the close-knit neighborhood dropped a stitch.

All she heard was, *"Mrs. McDonnell."*

She staggered as she stepped back from the open door, and the two marines immediately followed her into the living room, cautiously acting

77

out of fear that she might collapse. This would not be the last door they would reluctantly darken during this terribly dreadful war.

"*Dad, come out here. Come out here, now,*" Mom McDonnell called.

The two bearers of impending grief stood tall, one with the unread telegram gripped in his slightly trembling hand. No matter how hard he willed, he couldn't steel his uncooperative limb. The other marine was posed to speak.

Dad McDonnell walked nonchalantly into the room to find out what all the fuss was about. He was immediately startled by the presence of the two uniformed strangers staring back at him. His eyes went to his wife's, and hers went to his. Then they both looked blankly back to the uniforms.

He gave them a silent head-to-toe look and immediately fixated on the envelope one of the marine's held between the thumb and forefinger of his outstretched hand. Without a word, he reached out and took possession of the off-white envelope bearing his name and address.

"Sir."

Dad's openhanded gesture requested silence. His request was immediately honored.

"Please have a seat, gentlemen."

It was the very best he could offer. No other words were forthcoming. He started to open the envelope but abruptly stopped and turned to sit alongside Mom as his knees weakened. The marine's hand tremble had been transferred to Dad as he opened the ominous envelope.

Together, they read the telegram: *We regret to inform you … your son … Captain James McDonnell … killed in action …Southeast Asia …*

Dad, an extremely quiet man, now ashen with shock, belatedly looked up and directly into the pair of saddened and empathetic on looking eyes. He swallowed hard and choked with grief as he asked the terminal question, "Is this true?"

"I regret to inform you that, yes sir, yes ma'am, your son was killed in action."

The lower ranking member of the twosome followed suit. "Yes sir, he was."

The two marines immediately broke eye contact. God, how they hated this duty. They always saw their own parents looking back at them.

Mom, a tough cookie on the outside, began to weep but she stifled herself. *There'll be none of that*, she thought to herself. She stood, took control, and motioned for them all to follow her to the kitchen. That was the room for celebrating good news and sharing bad news. She proceeded to put on some coffee.

The three followed in pecking order and cautiously sat at the kitchen counter that Dad McDonnell had built with his own huge hands. Dad reached to a familiar spot underneath it for a bottle. He poured himself a long shot of bourbon and chased it with another. Ignoring the others momentarily, he promptly returned the bottle to its locker.

The two marines were at a loss. They looked about the unfamiliar surroundings, all the while purposely avoiding any form of eye contact. There was no nervous chatter, not a sound whatsoever other than the slight bone rattles of the steam pipes as the cellar furnace kicked in and the heat began to come up. The senior marine cleared his throat and announced that they would take their leave. Mom McDonnell rose and silently showed them to the front door. There was no further exchange of words. Upon hearing the front door close, Dad reached once again for the bottle of bourbon.

The two-story, four bedroom house on the South Side of Scranton had had its share of up and downs. Built in the early 1900s, this cherished location was the McDonnell family homestead. Dad McDonnell had been born in the house and bought it from his family after his parents passed away. Several of his siblings had lived there early on in their marriages. The house had been somewhat updated, but it had retained an invisible old sod warmth that was felt by all who visited. Dad had also acquired a dilapidated apartment building near the university that he had painstakingly renovated into a showplace. It was also the source of his income since being forced into early retirement due to cutbacks in senior personnel at his former place of employment.

In the early years, the McDonnell's house and yard had been a place of play for many of the neighborhood kids. In fact, the front porch and the rear patio were the main gathering places, and the kitchen a close third for those who managed to angle an extra place at the dinner table.

The Burke boys, the Holleran brothers, one of the Cappelloni kids, Straub, Malloy, Whalen, and Baldy from next door, along with young Mick from the other side, had been just some of the regulars. In addition, Lalley, Hannon, McIntyre, Kelly, Dunning, Wicker, Miles, and Murphy had been part of the scene as well. Nicknames such as Shorty, Faker, Moe, Rip, Chipper, Mook, Lefty, Mac, Chuck, Juba, and Butch had filled the air. At one time or another, most of the young guys from the melting pot neighborhood had hung out at McDonnells'.

If one of them had verbalized anything perplexing, Mom McDonnell had always presented a positive solution. It had been said that if the devil himself were to make an appearance, she could put a positive spin on hell itself.

During the most recent years, the homestead's sole occupants had been Mom, Dad, brothers Joe and Jim, and a stray pup named Blackie. The Irish twins, as the boys had often been referred to by others, had been inseparable. It had been said that as one brother was coming out of the womb, the other was swimming in. An ancient uncle who had come with the house had died some years earlier.

Joe had left the roost to begin a life on the edge and was now en route home, having been informed of his brother's death while he had also been on the other side of the world. His parents referred to Joe as being "overseas." Jim, on the other hand, had been temporarily serving in Vietnam.

Jim's temporary absence STOP with the delivery of a telegram STOP had just become permanent.

An excruciatingly long wait ensued until his body finally arrived home. The delay, though often questioned, was never explained to any family member's satisfaction. Throughout the delay, untold phone calls—both incoming and outgoing—were processed. A myriad of arrangements, not all of them necessary, had filled the hollow void echoing throughout the remaining family and friends.

Extended family and neighbors wore a path in and out of the house, solemnly delivering homemade food and baked goods. The short stays, always by women with uncharacteristically few words spoken, were accompanied out the door with twice-broken hearts and reams of streaming tears.

All of this activity would, no *must*, transpire before any time would be allotted to mourning by the McDonnells. Yes, that was the order of things, and Mom McDonnell saw to it with a dry eye. As for Dad McDonnell, he became even more silent. There were a lot of questions, though some were never asked and others that were quietly wondered aloud to no one in particular, that were never answered. That is just how things were from that point on in what was left of the now broken and emotionally crushed McDonnell family.

****

The final ride was a timeless void for the passenger. In this case, the beginning started with a South Vietnam infantry search and rescue crew reaching the crash site in multiple helicopters. They proceeded to secure the area, make the head count, do the mandatory checking of dog tag IDs, and grudgingly bag the remains.

It was a hell of a lot better than combat, but it was still a lousy duty. Once the body bags were moved to a suitable area, an evacuation helicopter arrived to begin the final "in country" ride, which would culminate with their arrival at Graves Registration within the Saigon morgue.

During that period of the war, the Saigon morgue operated around the clock. The malodorous air of the crowded work areas, though air-conditioned, permeated not only the nostrils but also into the skin and deep into the psyche of the assigned personnel. Most performed this dire but necessary duty admirably. However, tucked in among the occupied black plastic body bags and the neat stacks of bright aluminum caskets were more than a few two-legged rats that functioned with their own economic agenda.

Once the bodies were given their final prep, they were placed in a new body bag, zipped up tightly, and placed in a newly minted, military-issued metal casket. In many cases, the prep consisted of the gruesome task of placing various body parts into the bag and labeling the contents, *Sealed. Not for viewing. Do not open.*

Label or no label, the prepped cargo was ceremoniously loaded onto military transport planes for the first leg of a silent eastward-bound trip home. The first touchdown on American soil for a vast majority of those on their "final ride" was in Hawaii at the Kapalama Military Reservation. It was there, in a large World War II–era warehouse that had been converted into a temporary morgue, that the sorting took place for the various mainland military destinations that were closest to the dead warriors' homes.

The remains and personal property destined for the East Coast were flown to Dover Air Force Base in Dover, Delaware. The dense population of the Northeast dictated that a large number of young men and some women were either drafted and/or volunteered for military service. Thus, the inbound traffic to Dover was disproportionately heavy.

All the while, the families waited. Days grinded into weeks as concerned minds ran amok. Had there possibly there had been a mistake? Could that be the reason for the delay? Possibly! They prayed for some good news.

They pulled out all spiritual stops, and the praying began and, in many cases, never ended.

The local funeral director, a neighbor and friend of the McDonnell family, was given the necessary contact information by the marines for him to monitor the transport situation. He made his initial phone inquiry, left his contact information, and then went about his business. His business of death was practically an everyday activity, but this particular event was special because this funeral would be the first military funeral for one of "his own."

Rupert Beckley had known Jim as a kid in the neighborhood. His funeral home had annually sponsored the little league team Jim played on along with his brother, Joe. In later years, Rubert had been coerced into an additional sponsorship for the fledgling teener league. He had grown to enjoy the games.

Later on, both brothers had served as altar boys for funerals and still later fulfilled the roll of pallbearers for families in need of such assistance. Rupert recalled paying them the gratuitous sum of five dollars each for their services. He had been vocally proud of that gesture, and the boys had cherished the tips they each received.

From the onset of their first contact, the family called Rupert on a daily basis. Actually, Mom McDonnell made most of the calls. Rupert instructed his staff that he was to personally receive every call from the McDonnell family and that there was never ever to be any exception to this mandate. It was verbally carved in granite, and his staff complied without ever understanding the magnitude of Rupert's seemingly anal requirement.

This funeral was a big deal. As a local high school and college sports legend, Jim McDonnell was known all over the valley. Moreover, he had been one hell of a nice guy to boot. Top that off with him being a United States Marine Corps aviation officer that had died in Vietnam in the service of his country, and yeah, *this was a big deal.*

Other more prominent center city funeral directors would have welcomed the opportunity to serve the McDonnell family in their time of need. Even if it was at the expense of the small Rupert Beckley Funeral Home that was located smack dab in the middle of the neighborhood on the South Side of the city. Parking should have been a problem, but most people usually walked to the viewings at the "Corpse House."

Dot the *i*'s and cross the *t*'s. Rupert had his arms around the situation, and it was a death grip. The third week of waiting had just begun when

Rupert received the heads-up call. He had his newest Cadillac hearse unnecessarily washed and waxed for the second time in two days. Now it was time to roll, and everything else at the home was to be handled by his underlings, for Rupert was driving—by himself—nonstop to Dover and back. He was a man on a mission.

Rupert's round-trip return with the precious cargo was the spark that lit the short-lived fuse of emotional turmoil and speculation that ensued. It was late in the evening, but he felt obligated to inform the family that he had completed the trip without incident. He debated whether he should stop by the house or just phone. He decided to phone before it got too late in the day.

"Thank you for the call, Rupert. We'll be right over to see you," Mom McDonnell said.

"Oh no, that won't be necessary at this hour," Rupert insisted.

Rupert was tired, and his normally sharp ear missed the urgency in her voice. Mom McDonnell didn't want to see Rupert; she wanted to see her son.

"Rupert, what in God's name is the matter with you? I want to see my son, and I want to see him tonight."

"No, no, no … You don't understand, Mrs. McDonnell. There can't be any type of viewing. The … the body … Jim's body cannot be viewed. You just don't understand. For you see, you would not even be able to recognize him."

She was unrelenting as she turned the phone over to Dad McDonnell in order to regroup her rattled wits. "Joe, do something, damn it."

"Rupert, what's the problem?" Dad McDonnell spoke in an unaccustomed loud and firm voice, which did not go past Rupert. In fact, it hit him right in the face with its abruptness.

Dad McDonnell listened intently as Rupert repeated himself in his freshly mustered command voice. Dad held the phone so Mom McDonnell could hear the conversation repeated just as it had been told to her. Visibly agitated, she didn't buy any of it. Jim was her son, and she would not be denied. She had heard enough and forcibly grabbed the phone from Dad's loose grip, which he readily released to her.

"Rupert, who the hell are you to tell me that I cannot view my son? You know, this matter can be handled by any number of others."

As smack as Dad McDonnell's previous question had hit Rupert in the face, Mom McDonnell's verbal shot across the bow threatened Rupert in the wallet. Rupert needed authority, and he needed it fast. This funeral was a big deal, and he was not about to lose it to those directors waiting in the wings. He went formal in his response. "Mrs. McDonnell, by order of the United States Marine Corps, the remains contained herein are officially labeled *not for viewing.* If I were to permit you to do otherwise, we both would be violating a direct order from the marines."

The ensuing silence hung like a flag on a dank windless day. Then slowly and softly, as if not to disturb the dead, Mom McDonnell practically whispered into the phone, "Rupert, are you sure? Are you positively sure that that is *my son* that you have over there at the funeral home?"

Without hesitation, Rupert responded in the positive, "Mrs. McDonnell, the remains have been positively identified by the Marine Corps. There is no doubt. He was identified at the morgue. We have all of his personal belongings, including your letters from home. Yes. Yes, I can assure you, beyond the shadow of a doubt, that this is your son that we are soon to pray over and place into eternal rest."

Again, breathless silence ensued on both ends. "Well, if the marines say so." Mom McDonnell had just emotionally capitulated. In doing so, she mentally elevated the United States Marine Corps and dutifully placed them up on the narrow pedestal that until this very moment she had reserved solely for Catholic clergy and the local doctors. The Corps was now one of the chosen few and would remain as such for the balance of her life.

Her voice trailed off, and her lifelong bravado slowly but permanently deserted her in a painful departure that commenced with a slow single tear that ran unabatedly down the length of her cheek and disappeared into the pores of the phone.

She handed the phone back to her awestruck husband and firmly made the decision to go forward in another direction. She would now get overly busy with the final arrangements, and there would never ever be any mention of this conversation. As far as she was concerned, it had never happened.

Young Joe McDonnell arrived home in the dead of that eventful night. The front door, as he expected, was unlocked. Unexpectedly, the kitchen light was on, and his dad was quietly seated, staring off into another world.

Joe had winged his way across the Pacific in military transports. He had touched down in Okinawa, Hawaii, and finally California. At Camp Pendleton, he had received his paperwork releasing him from active duty and returning him to his reserve status to finish the final months of his military obligation. An honorable discharge would follow at that time.

It had been suggested by some that he conclude the domestic leg of his trip wearing civilian clothing. He was advised to do so to avoid public confrontation from the plethora of anti-war demonstrators that prowled public places, looking for boys in uniform. It had pissed him off, and he had worn his summer dress uniform out of spite.

God help the dumb bastard, male or female, young or old, that spat upon him. There would be blood on the walls, and very little of it would be his.

***

Joe dropped his sea bag and softly walked up from behind and put his hand on his father's slumped shoulder.

Without a glance, the older man welcomed his son. "Been expecting you."

Joe pulled out one of the old, worn chairs that had been part of the original kitchen table set before it had been replaced by Dad's new breakfast bar.

"How ya doing, Dad?" he asked.

His father's cigarette burned lightly, with a sagging inch of ash hanging in the balance. Joe moved the ash tray underneath it and, in the shadows of the overhead light, observed a fatal sadness in his father's body language. Dad had his hands cupped in front of him, and his head was at half-mast. There was no eye contact. It was as if he had been going somewhere far away, and his son's intrusion had interrupted the beginning of the journey.

"Want a drink?" Dad finally spoke as he reached down for the bottle that was underneath the counter where he sat transfixed and utterly devastated.

There was no glass in front of him, and thus Joe assumed that at least he hadn't been sitting there, drinking alone in the late of the night. That would have been out of character for his dad. Drinking alone at the house was something he had never observed his father do. The bottle was always available for friends and neighbors who dropped in. Of course, Dad always joined them in a drink.

"Yeah, Dad. I'll have a beer."

"There isn't any."

"Well, then I'll have a shot with you."

The greeting, the salutation, was over. There had always been few words that passed between them but lots of unspoken love. Joe was the opposite of his dad. His dad was a quiet and soft-spoken man who never made any waves. Joe, on the other hand, always made his presence known and had a tendency to be aggressive. He had never known if Dad disliked his demeanor or envied it.

He hated the smell, let alone the taste of whiskey. At one time, Dad had kept a top-shelf bottle of bourbon at the house, and that had been palatable in the past when they shared an occasional holiday boilermaker. However, for some unknown reason, Dad had switched to cheap off-brand whiskey. Mom suspected he did so because one neighbor in particular had begun to stop by far too often. Truth be known, Dad kept a bottle of each. Tonight though, he had already consumed the good stuff.

Joe's palette was in for a hard ride. The bottom-shelf bottle of rotgut and two jumbo shot glasses quietly surfaced, and Dad McDonnell proceeded to return to his previously inattentive position, burning cigarette still in hand. After a moment, Joe reached out and took charge of the process. He poured them each a good stiff one well past the white line on the glass, right up to the brim.

There was no clanking of the glasses. It was all Joe could do to keep from spilling the dark golden elixir onto his surrounding three-finger grip as he gingerly hoisted the over-full glass to his lips, gave it a quick sip, and then downed it in one practiced motion.

Good God! It was awful stuff. Joe practically gagged as the hot lava washed down his throat. Dad followed suit, although more adeptly. He then silently placed the glass down on his Formica countertop and, with a blackjack motion, called for another hit. Joe poured again but held his glass in reserve. Dad downed the second as smoothly as the first and then turned his head toward Joe and made eye contact.

"We lost our buddy."

"Yeah, Pop, we sure did."

With a singular exception, those were the only words they ever exchanged on the subject of Jim's death as Dad began his lonely, internal journey accompanied only by his memories. He never invited anyone else along for the ride.

Joe threw down his drink, swallowed it hard with an eye-squinting gulp, and sadly observed as the second member of the McDonnell family slowly began his lonesome pilgrimage toward death. It was to be a much shorter trip than his son Jim had just completed. He would be buried alongside his son across town in the family plot within two years. He would die of a broken heart, or so they would say.

Something weighed heavily on Joe's mind throughout the first of many sleepless nights that followed. His experiences of the past half-year would remain easily submerged from view because no one ever broached the subject, including his parents. However, paramount in his mind was a touchy subject—more for Mom rather than Dad—but he would have to have Dad's support to pull it off. His timing would be crucial.

The next day was Monday, and he waited until the evening. Sometimes the timing just isn't right and other times when you think it is perfect timing, it ain't. Dinner had passed quickly and quietly that evening. It was potluck from the numerous neighbors' drop-off menus. Joe helped clear the paper plates and plastic utensils, which surprised his mom. Then, before Mom and Dad could retire to the TV room, he carefully picked his words.

"Mom, Dad, I have something very important I'd like to discuss with the both of you."

Dad was seated in his favorite maple kitchen chair, and Mom immediately began fidgeting at the sink as if preparing to ward off evil spirits. Neither of them responded.

"Mom, please sit down here with Dad and listen to what I have to say. It will only take a minute or so."

Joe had no idea how short his minute would be, but nevertheless he jumped right in, soon placing both feet firmly in his mouth.

"Mom and Dad, years ago Jim and I had a very serious conversation, which he initiated, shortly after John F. Kennedy was assassinated and later buried in Arlington National Cemetery."

Mom McDonnell, now on alert because she loved to talk politics, moved to the edge of her chair as she spoke. "Kennedy was a good man, and he was the best darn Democrat that ever walked the face of the earth besides Franklin D. Roosevelt."

Dad McDonnell nodded his head in approval of Mom's brief emotional eulogy.

"Right, Mom. However, please let me continue. Jim and I were shooting pool at the Ukrainian Club, lost our game, and had to give up the table. We were sitting at the bar having a couple of Schaffer's and smoking Parodi cigars."

"You two had no sense when you got into the sauce," Mom said.

"No, Mom, we were quite sober." He continued, "An older newsreel came on the TV about the Kennedy funeral. We both watched it, and Jim turned to me and asked me to promise him something. Are you two listening?"

An impatient nod ensued from Mom, with nothing forthcoming from Dad.

"All right then, Jim asked me to promise him that if he was eligible when he died, I would see to it that he was buried at Arlington with full military honors. I would like to ask you two to honor his wish. I gave him my word that I would."

Dad looked to Mom as she abruptly rose up to her exaggerated five-foot height. She gave Joe the evil eye and forcefully pointed at him with her right index finger, which over time had arthritically curved inward. As she angrily waved her finger at him, she defiantly spoke her piece.

"Over my dead body!"

The room fell completely silent. She had fire in her voice, and it was no stranger to either one of them.

"You two had too much to drink, and you should not have been smoking those stinking ropes. I taught you to never make promises that you cannot keep." Her voice raised an octave as she stepped directly into Joe's space, her finger now aimed like a Kukri dagger at his heart.

"Jim will be buried across town in the family plot, and when my time comes, I will be placed right along side of him. There will be no more talk of John Kennedy, Arlington, or any place else. Promises be damned. *Over my dead body.*"

With her feathers thoroughly ruffled, she marched out of the kitchen and out of sight into the TV room as Joe stood in stunned silence. He turned to his dad to plead with upward turned palms.

Dad was a man of few words, and he spoke softly but firmly. "Joe, you heard your mother. You'll have to wait until she is six feet underground herself. Then you can do exactly what you should do and honor your brother's spoken word. You have my blessing. Keep your word, son. Many times it's all you got."

"Thanks, Dad."

"Drink?"

Joe begged off with a flat wave of the hand. He still had an aftertaste of the rotgut from the night before, and he would have no more.

"Suit yourself."

***

The "viewing" commenced Wednesday at the Beckley Funeral Home. It was referred to as a viewing out of habit. A closed wood-grained civilian casket now encased the sealed body bag.

The casket, draped in Old Glory and solemnly positioned at the far end of the tacky, rectangular main parlor, rested along with the remains of the diseased and awaited the start of the procession. The plethora of empty wooden folding chairs along the perimeter were soon filled.

The ritual was scheduled from 2:00 PM to 4:00 PM and 7:00 PM to 9:00 PM on both Wednesday and Thursday. The rosary was held at 8:00 PM each evening, which many visitors tried to avoid. The funeral and burial followed on Friday.

Who could have known half of the city would show up for the observances. The hours for each evening were extended with Mom McDonnell's blessing as the line stretched out around the block in both directions.

The overflow of flowers at Beckley's was only surpassed by the head count of the humble and the dignitaries that passed to relay their condolences—old friends, new friends, family, educators, former coaches, and strangers who knew the importance of putting in an appearance. There were fellow warriors in dress blues with snap salutes and the professional mourners dressed entirely in black who sat in back but never missed a beat.

The word *hero* was whispered by a few, and those few would forever be remembered along with the accompanying individual marine escort that had been assigned to ceremoniously guard the casket.

A brief Friday morning "last respects" viewing was followed by a solemn, high-profile vehicle procession from Beckley's to the church. The nearby McDonnell house lay empty in the church's shadow. After an ancient religious ritual in God's house, with tears flowing the cavalcade proceeded directly to the cemetery under the direction of the clergy rather than of Rupert. Actually, the clergy were always in charge.

Friday's procession from the church to the cemetery, with the flag-draped coffin visible through the large side windows in the lead vehicle, brought traffic to a halt. Pedestrians on the busy avenues idled in place to get a glancing, inquisitive view. Veterans offered slow, gentle salutes or stood silently with their caps held solemnly over their knowing hearts. For a brief passing moment, time stood reverently still on the thoroughfares leading to the cemetery. It appeared that the remaining half of the city was proffering its last good-bye.

Thank God, it wasn't raining. Most didn't think about the depressive, penetrating pale that rain brought to a funeral. The beautiful month of May had begun its third week, the ground was somewhat firm underfoot, and all the people that could had gathered on this silent, breezy yet sunny Friday morning in the heart of the century-old cemetery that housed some of the valley's finest. Another was about to be grudgingly added to the count. However, Joe harbored a gnawing doubt about his brother's death that he silently held close to his heart. It would be some time before he could act upon it. When he did, he would seek answers from the Marine Corps, but none would ever be forthcoming.

The conclusion of the burial ceremony began with the sprinkle of holy water upon the flag-draped casket and a few more *amens*. No one was prepared for "Taps," and even the stalwarts began to cry. All but one person recoiled at the sounding report of the multi-gun salute. The folding of Old Glory into a neatly tucked, star-spangled triangle and the passing of the "colors" to Mom McDonnell signaled the end of the brief military ceremony.

A blurred retracing of their steps led them homeward. It was an adrenaline-driven forced march, and the McDonnells never missed a step. There would be time for that later when the adrenaline was replaced with alcohol. However, their next focus was on the folks that were invited back to the McDonnell homestead for the balance of the Irish wake. An Irish wake that, for Mrs. and Mr. McDonnell, would have no end.

Chapter 15

Good Lord, these guys stink. Wild Bill could no longer stand the stench in the confines of his office. He buzzed a subordinate and arranged to swap vehicles with him.

They strode out the door into the late afternoon sun and proceeded two by two toward several vehicles. Bill hopped into the driver's seat of a faded yellow pickup truck while motioning to the others. "You guys, ride in the back."

With the others in tow in the rear bed, he drove directly to the Base Exchange and invited them inside. Bill immediately organized a brief spree. The BX had multiples of most basics, and Bill arranged for the ragged three to be outfitted, by local standards, to the nines. Bags in hand, they proceeded back to the truck.

They felt a hell of a lot better, but they were still in a quandary about their eventual fates. Hank was slightly sullen, Jim was somewhat cautiously upbeat, and Thatch, well, he was undergoing a metamorphous that had yet to unravel.

With a slow coast, they motored through the main gate at Udorn, past the Thai guard, and down the two-lane road toward Tikattanon Road. Then following a few zigs and zags, the backward ride stopped in front of the Paradise. The three men looked at each other as if to say, *the easy part of the ride is over, and now it's time for the inevitable interrogation.*

"Another drink would sit real well right about now," Jim said. He had a way of breaking the ice with his wit that the others were now beginning to expect from him. They looked his way and tilted their heads in agreement.

In short order, they were in separate rooms, and each had received the same set of instructions from Bill: "Meet me in the bar in twenty minutes." Each had a black-faced digital watch to go along with their newly acquired khaki shorts, slacks, dark brown sandals, collared shirts, and various and sundry accessories. In the bottom of the ninth, Bill had thrown in three baseball caps for good measure. The caps were the only items they had worn on the ride leading up to their inauspicious arrival at the Paradise Hotel.

The three guests completed the three *s*'s, leaving open for debate which they enjoyed the most. Within the allotted twenty minutes, they returned to the first floor of the multi-storied building that appeared to house approximately sixty rooms plus a dining room and a bar. It was in the bar that they rejoined Bill.

"Well, you three clean up real nice," Bill said.

"Thanks, Bill," all three men echoed.

Bill finished his drink, looked them over from head to toe again, and offered nothing but, "Let's go for another ride."

"Shit," Hank uttered. "I left my hat in the room."

With a certainty only Bill would know, came an assurance, "You won't need it."

The other two, for some unknown reason, had stuffed the caps in their rear pockets. They now placed them on their heads as the foursome departed the hotel lobby.

Bill was now in the possession of a four-door sedan, and the ISUZU was nowhere in sight. Once aboard they passed the heart-shaped swimming pool across from the hotel and merged forcefully into a light maze of two and four wheel traffic. After a bit, they partially circled the clock tower located on a traffic circle and headed straight for some yet-unknown pleasure. Bill intended to be the perfect host and at the same time have a little well-earned R&R for himself. He felt, rightfully so, that they had all earned some downtime. Their mystery destination was the Oscar Massage. Hank was in no mood for anything other than the massage.

Later, back at the Paradise, Bill suggested that Hank and Jim catch a few winks before dinner.

"Bill, what time do you want to meet for dinner?" Jim asked. He certainly didn't want to sleep through a meal, but Bill's response didn't answer Jim's question.

"I don't know yet. It'll be up to you three as to what time we finally get to eat. I'm going to talk with Thatch right here at the bar, and then

I'll come up and visit individually with each of you. Go and relax. I'll get around to you after a bit."

It sounded a little ominous to Jim and Hank, but Thatch kind of expected it. He headed straight toward the bar ahead of Bill. Halfway up the first flight of stairs leading from the lobby, Jim turned to Hank. Placing his left hand on Hank's shoulder, he spoke his mind. "Hank, I can't believe you're still standing. If I had lost my family earlier today, I would be a basket case."

"Just what is it that leads you to believe that I am not just that? A basket case, as you put it, *mon ami?*"

"Then tell me, friend, is there anything I can do to help ease your suffering," Jim asked.

They were stopped on the first landing and Hank threw him a curve ball. "I have seen so much death and suffering that I am practically immune to it. Yes, I miss my wife and children, but I never should have had those beautiful moments in the ordinary course of my life; therefore, I can only count my blessings and then try to move on as best I can."

Jim listened and felt that something was fermenting within Hank. "That's it, Hank? Just move on?"

"No, Jim, that's not just it. By move on, I mean move on to the next confrontation. I will avenge my losses at the expense of others who will come, probably in the near future, and attempt to take precious things away from me. I don't know just who they might be, but I can assure you that I will know them when they come, and I will be prepared for them. Even if it costs me my life, I will go down fighting. I should have died in that hellhole that I left behind in Vietnam. As God is my judge, I will never walk away from a battle again."

In a prophetic way, Jim brought the conversation to an end, "Hank, someday I'll write that on your grave marker."

"It's too long to fit on a grave marker."

"Naw, Hank. The last sentence will fit just fine."

"I suppose it will."

"Now, Mr. Hank, let's get some shuteye before the 'bad cop' knocks on our doors."

"Bad cop?"

"Forget it."

Downstairs at the bar, Bill was quick with Thatch. He knew most of his story, and Thatch was extremely forthcoming with the rest of it. Now Bill knew that both Hank and Jim were aware not only of Thatch's mission but the purpose of it. *This is not good*, he thought. No, it certainly was not good. Those two were outsiders, and outsiders meant problems. It could only go one of two ways. They could be eliminated, which was an everyday occurrence around these parts, or they needed to join in and not be on the endangered species list of outsiders. Bill would hold all further thoughts until after speaking to them.

Bill instructed Thatch that they would have dinner in the hotel dining room around 8:00 and suggested he first look in the bar for him. Thatch went ahead of Bill to his room, not daring to stop and speak with his companions.

Bill flipped a lucky silver dollar that he had carried practically around the world since joining the agency. Hank unknowingly won, and Bill headed toward Hank's room.

W.B. Coade had lost count of which time at bat this would be for him. Interrogating people was second nature for him, and he felt no pressure. In reality, if he didn't like what he heard from Hank or Jim or if he wasn't sure of them in any way, they would just have to disappear. They wouldn't even make it to dinner. The bad cop was on his way.

Hank was ready for him. Verbally, he was prepared to fully cooperate with Bill. *What the hell*, he thought. *I've got nothing to hide and nothing to fear.* On the physical side, he figured he could wipe the room up with Bill. However, after beating the crap out of Bill, what the hell would he do for an encore? Hank began to mentally review his situation.

He was isolated in a strange country with unknown customs, and he had no papers or any type of identification in hand. His only salvation was Bill, and Hank was no dummy. Getting physical should be the very last move to make at this time. He decided he would just sit tight and wait to see what Bill had to offer.

Bill knocked once, and Hank immediately let him in. They moved directly into the bright room and sat opposite each other in undersized upholstered chairs with a small table between them. Bill rose and moved his chair so that they could view each other more easily. Hank had his back to the window, and Bill was closest to the door.

"Hank, please tell me about yourself. You know, in a big picture kind of way. Let's start with just how you ended up in southern Laos, and we'll just go on from there."

Hank began to tell his story, and Bill absorbed the warrior's tale with growing respect. With few interruptions from Bill, the timeline flowed from Hanoi to hell on earth at Dien Bin Phu, life on the trail, the annihilation of his family, the total destruction of their small village, and the battle to save it. Bill was intrigued by the battle-ready preparations Hank had undertaken in anticipation of an attack.

This guy was his kind of guy, and Bill determined that Hank could lend a good hand in the secret war that was going on north of them in Laos. His only concern was that he didn't think Hank would follow any kind of orders. He was a wild card, but he could make a good hand. Hank was a keeper if the rest of the "visit" followed in the same straightforward vein.

"Tell me about Jim. What do you know of him?"

Oh boy, thought Hank. He hadn't thought about this line of questioning. He logically figured it would be directed at Jim himself during his time in the barrel with Bill. "I guess I thought wrong," Hank said without realizing he had verbalized his final thought aloud.

"Say what, Hank?

"Oh, nothing, Bill."

Bill pursued the opening. "Thought wrong about what, Hank?"

Hank hesitated briefly and then spoke up, "Shit. I've got a decision to make."

"Make the right one, Hank. Up until now, you've been doing just fine." Bill reached into his back pocket and pulled out a leather-wrapped flask he carried as a survival kit. Taking a quick nip, he offered it to Hank.

"It's thirty-year-old single malt Scotch, if that means anything to a Frenchman."

"Yeah, it means that it's just about as old as I am."

Bill then countered. "Obviously a damn good year. Let's not spoil it at this stage of the game."

Hank took a sniff and then a sip. He followed it with a long draw. Bill's words of wisdom were not lost on him. With his nerves somewhat steadied, Hank leaned back in the uncomfortable chair, with his head tilted up toward the ceiling. He savored his mouthful of Scotch before slowly swallowing it. After regaining eye contact with Bill, Hank loosened up.

"Ya know, Bill, Jim can speak for himself, but ... I fear you're not going to let me off the hook that easily."

"Not on your life. You are still on the hook! However, I will tell you this. What we discuss about Jim will stay in this room, and just so you understand, I'm going to ask Jim the same question about you. So if we have missed anything significant, I suggest you get it out on the table before I leave the room, and I do not want to debate the meaning of the word *significant*." Bill paused a moment to let his pronouncement deliver its full effect and for the thirty-year-old single malt to settle in. "Now tell me, what about Jim?"

Hank was weighing empty air. He was damned if he did and damned if he didn't. Should he continue to lie about Jim's background? Jim certainly was in no position to contradict him. However, this was the CIA. Jim had flown them into Thailand. If Bill somehow checked out Jim, how would Hank perpetuate the lie? Then, if caught in the devilish lie, both Bill and Jim would be all over him. It was time to come clean.

"Jim doesn't know who he is."

"I'm aware of that, Hank." Bill's sarcasm was obvious and betrayed his impatience.

"Things are not exactly as they appear, Bill. If the truth is to be known, I know Jim's true identity." There, he had said it. It was off his chest, and he was now mentally prepared to let the other shoe drop. "I've deceived him. I told him that I thought he was a deserter from the American military. I kept his true identity from him for selfish reasons. Bill, basically, I'm ashamed of what I have done."

"Hank, cut to the chase. What the hell have you done?"

Hank ruefully reached into the pocket of his new slacks and produced a single dog tag. He held it out for Bill to peruse and asked for another drink from the flask.

The U.S. military dog tags came in pairs strung on a chain worn around the neck. In death, one of the pair stayed with the body, and one went to those remaining in authority who would document the loss in a summary report. In Jim's case, Hank had been the reigning authority and had copped the second tag at the crash site on the night he had found Captain James McDonnell.

Bill zeroed in on the name and serial number stamped on the thin metal tag. Then he observed the religion and blood type. The first digit of the serial number, a zero, told him Jim was an officer. Right now, that was Jim's whole life story, but Bill was armed to the teeth, and the door to the information barn was now wide open. He caressed the tag between his thumb and forefinger and handed Hank the flask after taking a quick snort himself.

The clock ran on as Hank gave Bill every detail, including his deceptive move with the ID tag exchange and the flight suit change with the dead Vietnamese prisoner. Jesus, the more Bill heard, the more he began to admire Hank's instincts. That was it. Hank passed muster. In some way, shape, or form, he was going to join the team. In what manner would be a question for another day.

"Hank, the part of this conversation concerning Jim *never took place,* got it? Nothing passed between us other than the Scotch, got it? Now, go and get your partner in crime and join us down at the bar for a drink before dinner.

"Jim?"

"Yes, Hank, Jim. I'll talk with him tomorrow while you cool your jets at the pool. Everything will be A-OK. I'll take good care of you boys."

With that, Bill rose to leave the room and abruptly turned as he stopped short at the door. "Oh, one more thing, Hank. Hand me my flask. I need to refill my little friend. He can't run on empty."

Hank followed Bill out the door and into the dim hallway. He turned left and headed directly to Jim's room, which was conveniently located four doors down the hall. His quick knock was followed by a quick response.

"Hello, Jim. Expecting someone else?"

"No, Doctor Livingston, I was expecting you all along. Won't you please come on in?"

"No way, Jim. Bill is expecting us to join them downstairs now."

"What the hell is wrong with you?" Jim detected Hank's anxiety and was immediately concerned for him.

"No problem, Jim. I just had a drink or two with Bill and filled him in on my background."

"Hmmm. How did it go? Any mention of me?"

"No, not really. He wanted to know if we knew about Thatcher's adventure. A simple yes seemed to satisfy him. I guess a lot of that dope stuff takes place around here, and no one thinks much about it. But what the hell do I know? Let's eat."

Jim smelled a rat. Something just didn't sit right with him regarding Hank's demeanor. He went on full alert and cautiously nursed his drinks throughout the late dinner that long but uneventful evening at the Paradise Hotel.

Chapter 16

As one side of the world wrestles with sleep, the other side tackles its daily tasks. W.B. "Bill" Coade was no stranger when it came to working both sides of the street.

His true name was William Burke Coade, and as a young kid, he had informed all who would listen that he was a direct descendent of the famous Wild Bill Cody—the one and only "Buffalo Bill Cody" that had shot up the west and later the stage as a performer in Wild West shows that toured the United States. When challenged about the spelling of his last name, Bill would retort with the proclamation that his family had changed the spelling of their name from Cody to Coade many years ago. He never gave a reason why such a change had been made, and the few times he was challenged, he had concocted a further explanation that had always seemed to suffice.

Basically, Bill had grown up leading the life of an army brat, following his divorced father all over the world. He never really had any roots, and so home was literally wherever he hung his hat. Later in life, after a stint with U.S. Army Intelligence, he had joined the elite ranks of the CIA. His mother and father had passed away over the ensuing years, and he had truly become a lone wolf. He feared no one, usually rattled the wrong cages at CIA headquarters, and had eventually ended up at Udorn as the CIA agent-in-charge (station agent) of the entire operation of the secret war in Laos. He was uniquely qualified to lead the pack.

He had presented himself in a multitude of interesting and life-challenging places around the world, with dozens of covert cover identifications and occupations that involved a myriad of assignments. Many times, Bill had been on the edge of being uncovered only to mysteriously leave town just before his exposure would result in the director disavowing all knowledge of his existence.

He had fulfilled most of his assigned goals, to boot, and had received rave reviews from the powers at be at CIA headquarters in Langly, Virginia. His only problem was that he really had a way of pissing off each and every one of those same people. However, they respected him as a person, though from a distance.

While Bill and his three guests endured a late dinner, Bill already had wheels turning halfway across the world. Through the American embassy in Vientiane, Laos, he had initiated an inquiry as to the status of Captain James McDonnell. The inquiry, which included the captain's military serial number, would be extremely circuitous, and by the time it reached Langly, it had all the appearances of originating from a major life insurance company headquartered in Hartford, Conn. A friend at Langly casually forwarded the inquiry to the U.S. State Department and the Department of Veterans Affairs, and by day's end, the information was securely in the hands of inquiry's originator, the paper trail was destroyed, and no one would be the wiser.

Now, what the hell do I do with this? Bill sat at his desk the next day. It was another busy morning at Udorn, and he had just finished reviewing and responding where necessary to the overnight dispatches that littered his desk. He burned all but one two-page document in his large metal waste basket and turned his attention to the remaining document as his office partially filled with smoke. He casually carried the smoldering basket out into the hallway and left it for others to deal with.

An aide rushed from an adjoining office to remove the smoldering threat from the building—a morning ritual—as an almost ghostlike figure emerged through the partially smoke-filled hallway.

"Good morning, Bill." It was Jim McDonnell.

Bill had been expecting Jim since he had earlier directed an aide to pick up and deliver Jim from the Paradise.

"Come on in, stranger. Glad you could make it. Some coffee?"

Stranger, hmmm, that's indeed an off-the-cuff greeting, Jim thought. *This ought to be interesting.*

Jim poured himself a cup of black coffee from the small universal table along the wall behind and to the left of Bill's desk and, without waiting for an invitation, seated himself in the same chair he had briefly occupied the day before. Bill followed suit, and they were both seated as they had been the day before—directly opposite each other. A prolonged silence followed while Bill pretended to review the two pages of information he held before him. He then placed the document flat on his desk so that only the large diagonal gray stamp imprint was easily readable by Jim. It read, *Classified. Destroy after reading.*

What the hell is this? thought Jim, as he sipped the lukewarm coffee and waited for Bill to make his anticipated move. Bill did not disappoint him.

"Well, captain, welcome back."

If the chair had had rockers, it would have involuntary started in motion. Jim leaned forward and placed his coffee cup off to the side of Bill's desk. Then, sitting back and placing both elbows on the wooden arms of the chair, he moved his praying symbol hands to his pursed lips and stared directly into Bill's brain.

What's going on in there? I can see his wheels turning, but he's not giving me anything. Don't say a word. Wait him out. I've got plenty of time and nowhere to go. I'll just wait him out. That was the sum of Jim's thoughts. He didn't have to wait long.

"I see I have your interest, and I won't play any games with you."

"Bill, I think you've already begun the game. Let's play it and finish it in a timely manner."

"Okay, Jim, I owe you that much. I have before me a dossier that outlines your background and tells me exactly who you are. I cannot show it to you, but I can sure as hell read it to you."

Bill rose, refilled his cup, and topped off Jim's. He began to speak before being seated. "Here we go." Bill proceeded to read from the top, delivering the full name, rank, military branch, and serial number. He followed with date of birth and place of birth and then looked up at Jim. "Mean anything to you?

"Nope, not a damn thing. Please go on."

"Okay, then."

Bill had decided much earlier in the day just how this discovery would proceed. Once he had read that Jim was "prematurely dead and buried," he had chuckled to himself over a familiar quote attributed to Mark Twain. At the same time, Bill was a pragmatic man. He needed an experienced gunship pilot for TN, and he didn't want any Thai pilot getting up close and personal with his general. If anyone was going to fly the general around the Plain of Jars, or anywhere else in Laos for that matter, it was going to be one of his own guys. He was hell-bent for leather on that guy being Jim McDonnell.

Much in the same vein of his Buffalo Bill concoctions, Bill was about to weave one of his craftiest creations. To suit his endgame, Bill was now going to fabricate the big picture of Jim's life right up until the time he crashed his Huey in the jungle along the Ho Chi Minh trail. At the same time, he was going to keep his word and prevent any fallout from landing on Hank's head, for he had given Hank his word. In addition, he wanted Hank on his side.

Thus, he continued, "Captain Jim, it says here, you were born in Brooklyn, New York. You were the only child of a career navy enlisted man. Your mother and father were divorced when you were ten years old, and she eventually remarried, moved somewhere in the midwest United States, and later died. There is no known record of her place of burial. You lived with your father at various navy bases around the world. Your father died when you were eighteen, and you joined the marines. Your father's remains were cremated and spread only God knows where.

"You have no known living relatives. You served in various locations with the marines and received your GED while on active duty. Eventually you were awarded an undergraduate degree while an officer candidate. You successfully completed flight school at Pensacola, and your next stop was Vietnam. Any questions?"

"No."

"Remember any of this at all?"

"No. I don't remember one iota of it. I'm at a complete loss."

"Shall I continue?"

"Absolutely. How the hell did I get from Vietnam to Hong Tre?"

"Well, Jim, at least you still remember Hong Tre and the events leading up to today. Hopefully over time you will begin to recall the rest of your life."

"Yeah, well, at least I can hope so."

Jim felt overwhelmed with information that meant absolutely nothing to him. It was all emotionless dribble. It just did not mean a damn thing to him, and it was a lousy feeling that egged him on. "Again, how did I get to Hong Tre from Vietnam?"

Before answering, Bill abruptly rose and turned to adjust the temperature control on the wall-mounted air conditioner located directly behind him. It was beginning to get warm in his office.

"You were on a special mission into Laos to pick up a North Vietnamese prisoner." Bill started his dialogue with his back to Jim and continued as he turned and sat slowly down in his well-worn chair that was growing more uncomfortable by the minute. "Your Huey was shot down, and it crashed and burned. As best it can be determined, from the summary reports, your body was recovered along with the other crew members and returned stateside. Your personal papers contained a last will and testament requesting cremation with your ashes scattered off shore at Pensacola. Since you had no next of kin, your other assets, as directed, were donated to various veterans associations."

"Christ, Bill, you mean that as far as the world is concerned I'm dead and buried?'

"Yup, that's exactly what I'm reading."

"Then how the hell am I here, alive and well, sitting directly in front of you?"

"Well, here's what is not in the report. Your friend Hank found you on the trail in a state of unconsciousness."

"That I know."

"Now, somehow you survived and wandered away from the crash site but not before you did something clever that covered your tracks. Obviously, the head count added up for the search and rescue party, and since you're not wearing your dog tags, it can be assumed that you left them behind with or without your knowledge. Granted, that's a big assumption, but it's the only conclusion I can draw."

Jim offered a quick question. "You know that I was dressed in peasant garb when Hank found me?

"Yes, I do, and that is why Hank assumed you were a deserter trying to cover your tracks while, as I said, I think you were damn clever and attempting to avoid capture. You can draw your own conclusion."

"Oh Christ, at this juncture I don't know what the hell to think."

"Don't spend any time thinking about anything. I've been around, and I've got to tell you the last thing you need to do is go thinking about this situation. Accept what has happened, and ask yourself if you are better off now than you were before."

"What the hell do you mean?" Jim was getting flustered.

"Well, come on, Jimbo. You were drop-shipped into a shitty war that is being run by a bunch of assholes that have no intention of ever winning. They're treading water while dangling you and your ilk as bait."

"That's your take, Bill, and it doesn't sound very patriotic."

"Patriotic my ass. You want patriotic? I'll give you patriotic. Laos is patriotic. We're winning in Laos. We're defeating the damn communists. I think Vietnam will fall on its ass, but Laos will forever stand as a democratic nation. Do you want to know why I feel that strongly about this war?"

"Yeah, damn it. That is something I would like to hear." Jim felt more than just a little hostile as his heart began to pound in his chest.

"The eggheads that are in charge in Vietnam are not really running the damn show. The American ambassador in Saigon is calling the shots. In addition, do you know who is filling up his head? There's a bunch of guys in Washington that don't know shit from whatever about winning a goddamn war." Bill was just warming up, and for decorum sake, it was best that he had not yet begun to drink that day.

"Jim, I like and respect you. So let me tell you something that, to the best of my knowledge I've never said aloud to anyone. The American ambassador in Vientiane, Laos, thinks he is running this here war. Well, I'm here to tell you that he can think any damn thing he wants to think. Nevertheless, the thing of it is, damn it, I'm running this frigging war. I call the shots, and I make things happen. As for the ambassador, he can kiss my green Irish ass."

Jim was somewhat aghast. Here he was a by-the-book kind of guy. Yes, he harbored a little pent-up what-they-don't-know-won't-hurt-them kind of attitude that whispered in his ear every now and then, but this was way over his head. To the best of his short memory, he'd never had access to someone this high up the totem pole, and coupling that with his total apolitical view of the Vietnam War, his mental wheels began to lose traction.

Then, seizing the moment, Bill unknowingly added some glue that would help seal the deal that he would soon propose. "One additional thing, Jim. If any son of a bitch that works for me wants to march in that door unannounced and get in my face over any goddamn order I issue, he's more than welcome to do so. They may have to carry him out of here on a litter, but you can bet your young ass he will understand exactly what I am doing and how I intend to do it. Moreover, you know what? That bastard will go out there, he will follow those orders, and he will get the job done. Now, you try that shit in your damn Marine Corps."

Jim was almost on total overload. He was receiving too much information in too short a time. After taking several deep breaths, his heartbeat slowed, but his head spun. Then, without a further thought, he spoke up and took the bait. "Bill, as I see it, I'm at a broad fork in a crooked road, and it's just the two of us walking and talking."

The phone came to life, and Bill answered and responded, "Yeah, I'm ready."

Lunch arrived promptly, as if the phone call had just been made from the hallway outside of Bill's office door. Jim looked at his watch and noted it was only 11:00 AM.

The sharp young guy, who was obviously not one's typical gopher, set the tray on the edge of the universal table. He cleared the coffee apparatus and replaced it with a bottle of Scotch and some sliced sandwiches. The coffee table was now the bar. Jim observed and wondered what the hell else that damn table was used for. Meanwhile, the aide replaced the wastebasket and quietly closed the door as he exited the room.

"Jim, we were walking, and you were talking. Please continue."

"Bill, as I see it I've got two options. Option one, with your assistance, I head back to Uncle Sam in Vietnam and explain what has happened to me." Jim paused to think about what he had just not said. *How the hell in the world am I going to rationally explain this total snafu?*

"And option two, Jim?"

"Option two, Bill, is that I stay here and help fight this war—your war—and see where it all washes out afterward, you know, in the end."

"You only think you have two options, Jimbo." Bill intentionally used Jim's long-time nickname as he got up and took a bite of a half sandwich and offered the other half to Jim, which he accepted. Then, Bill—being Bill—poured a glass of Scotch.

"I never drink on an empty stomach unless I have to."

He motioned to Jim with an empty glass in hand, but Jim declined. Bill poured him one anyway, and Jim accepted. Then he immediately placed the drink on Bill's desk among the numerous water ring stains.

"You'll want that before I finish." Bill was back at his desk, sipping his scotch and ready to strike while the iron was hot. "Jim, I've got ten or more years on you in age, and in those ten years, I've condensed more knowledge about people and bureaucracies than you ever will, even if you live to be one hundred." Bill didn't wait for a response. He didn't want one just yet.

"Now Jim, let's discuss option one. Here's why that won't work for you. Say I get you back in touch with the Marine Corps. Here's the buzz saw that's going to cut the legs right out from under you. First, they flat out will not believe you. Forget about the scenario of you being alive, then being dead, and now you're back in their world once more alive. Also, let's for the moment forget about who *they* are and concentrate on just what *they* will do.

"There will be redundant mental exams to determine whether your condition is fatigue—that is mental, for the record—or if you're just some kind of deserter that faked his death and now wants back in the game. Then you know what, bucko, *they* are going to take the safe way out and declare you unfit for duty due to physiological reasons. Then some board of jerks will agree unanimously with the finding, and you will be out on the street in a flash. You'll have in your possession a medical discharge and a free pass to a VA mental ward. You'll get some mustering out pay, but in no time, you won't have a dime in your pocket. I've already informed you that you have no family, and there'll be no normal identification papers because you don't really know who the hell you are other than what I just told you this morning."

Bill finished his first drink of the day. His throat was dry, and his now-clasped hands were a little sweaty. He got up and again adjusted the air conditioner.

"Bill, that option sounds like a lonesome walk down a short dark path to self destruction," Jim said. He realized they were both on the road walking and talking, but Bill was the only one making any sense.

Jim was chewing the bait and about to wash it down with a swallow of Scotch when Bill sat back and observed him processing. Jim was a quick study. He took things at face value when he had to and made his decisions accordingly.

"Bill, it readily appears to me that the local option is the only option for me. Is it indeed an option that is on the table as we speak?"

"Jim, I have an option for you that will blow your socks off, but I'm waiting on some information that will determine when you come onboard."

"Are you talking about Air America?"

"No. This will be a private undertaking that will place you inside the heart and soul of this war. There is risk involved, but I assure you that you can make as much out of this as your little heart can stand. Basically, it's a hotshot pilot's dream come true. Let's call it a done deal. You'll be on the payroll as of today, but you will have to wait awhile for things to catch up. You'll see. You'll see very soon. For now, let's call it a done deal."

Bill stood to indicate that he had given Jim all the time he was going to get this morning. Without a second thought, he separated the two sheets of paper he had just paraded in front of Jim, lit one afire and casually dropped it into his eternally charred waste basket. He handed the other sheet to Jim. Jim took a long look at a copy of his death certificate, glanced once at the smoldering basket, and stood.

He carefully twice folded the paper in hand and slid it into his left front shirt pocket. Leaving the balance of his drink on Bill's desk, he stood and shook hands with his proposed new boss across the desk. He then turned and headed to the door. While still gripping the knob, he hesitated. In an unexpected turn toward Bill, Jim gave him an inquisitive look while now halfway out the door. "Bill, I know that you are CIA and all that implies, but I have one more question for you."

Bill came around his desk as if to escort Jim the rest of the way out the door, but he stopped, leaving some maneuvering space between them.

"Shoot, Jim. What's the million dollar question?"

"How did you manage to get all that information about me when you only had my first name and my handle of Jimbo? Tell me, just how on earth did you accomplish that task practically overnight?"

Bill stood before Jim with his right hand deep in the front pocket of his trousers. He nervously fingered Jim's thin metal dog tag with his thumb and index finger. The ensuing silence broke when Bill's unconscious glance toward the floor met Jim's steady gaze.

Responding with a confidence that concealed the con, Bill looked directly into Jim's steely blue eyes and said, "Prints, Jim. Yeah, your fingerprints. I had your fingerprints lifted from your Scotch glass yesterday afternoon after we left here together. My boys then did what we get paid to do. We find things out."

The deal was sealed with this final prevarication. This newly forged union would endure, but it was not a match made in heaven. War—any war—was hell, and they both damn well knew that.

Chapter 17

The Laotian capital city of Vientiane was laced with French influence that was left over from so many years of colonial rule. Like many capital cities throughout the world, it also had its share of, among other things of interest, intrigue.

General TN had not been born into the upper echelons of local political society. That was reserved for a group of families whose influence touched practically every ruling facet of day-to-day life in Laos.

No, TN wasn't born into this sphere. He was raised by a poor Catholic family that had found solace in their religion. The church educated TN, and at the age of seventeen, he had entered the local seminary, where he stayed for three years studying to become a Catholic priest. However, a scandal of Tang's creation that could not be covered up forced him to quietly leave the seminary. He left unscathed and took with him an enviable education that served him well after he joined the military to escape poverty. Through cunning and new connections, over time he cracked barrier after barrier as he rose up through the ranks of the Laotian military. Tang was not the top general in Laos. He had been given the title of general to keep him wound up. The rank also kept his senior, General Ptope, totally removed from any and all matters having to do with active war. He was a total figurehead that was well ingrained within the lines of the controlling bluebloods.

General Ptope was not one to get his hands dirty with matters dealing with the communists from Vietnam, the local Pathet Lao, his own fractured military, and least of all the Americans and their alter ego, the CIA.

Thus, to keep everything copacetic, General TN was fronted as the go-to guy for matters dealing with the secret war. If things went bad, it would be his lonesome ass tied across the railroad track. As things were turning out, the war was going very well, and Lord, did the general milk the opportunity. General TN had sliced out for himself a massive piece of political clout that had the Vientiane political crowd kissing his ass, and the guileful general knew that the clock was always ticking on his fifteen minutes of fame.

***

When TN had left Bill's office and delayed meeting Thatch for an additional day, it had caught Bill a little off guard because he knew the importance of the information Thatch was carrying. What Bill would find out within the hour that day was that his friend TN was on his way to Vientiane for an overnight meeting with the political powers to be, to rub elbows and throw some bravado around.

TN was always testing the waters. He did not trust General Ptope, whom he considered a sympathizer with the communists, both at home and outside Laos. He had no respect for the American ambassador who honestly believed that every directive he signed off on was actually carried out as directed. The politicos, to TN, were just that. His presence made them feel important, and TN was well aware of the importance of that.

General TN had the world by the balls, and he knew it. However, the main reason he was in Vientiane for the evening was to engage in a previously arranged liaison that he had clandestinely arranged through a priestly friend.

TN was a pedophile, and he liked young boys. This highly guarded secret was masked by his practice of entertaining his contacts at various and sundry brothels on a regular basis. The general had a reputation as a real ladies' man, but just the opposite was true. TN was totally unaware of the fact that Bill had a dossier a mile long on him.

Bill also knew that his friend TN was planning to move big time into the lucrative drug environment. TN had dipped his toe into the drug pool a year ago and reaped enough to finance his upscale lifestyle. Bill now reckoned TN was gearing up to go all out into the drug trade business and eliminate any type of middleman. Thus, the recent heavy-handed demand that Bill was in the process of accommodating for the startup airline equipment and pilots. Bill was going to accommodate TN, but he would steadfastly maintain an arm's length distance from this dirty business. He was in the intelligence business, and it was not beyond him to step broadly over the line, but when it came to drugs, W.B. Coade was not of that ilk.

Just as General TN was looking boldly at the drug trade to finance his grandiose retirement scheme, Bill also had a scheme. However, unlike the general, Bill needed some special people behind the scenes to pull off his retirement plan.

The cauldron was not quite full just yet, but the principle ingredients were being gathered as TN returned to Udon the next day for his scheduled dinner with Thatch Pittsford at promptly eight o'clock in the evening.

Everything had gone exactly as planned in Vientiane, and the unsavory TN had satisfied his social and physical desires with gusto. Additionally, he was expecting his buzz to carry over into this evening, for disappointment was not something the diminutive man handled very well, and most people were keenly aware of that trait.

Chapter 18

The evening dinner at the Paradise brought some of the loose ends together. General TN received the long-delayed banking account information from Thatch. They reached an understanding that in return for this information, Thatch was back on the A-list. There would be no repercussions over the sojourn that had delayed his return to Udorn.

Bill offered Jim the pilot's job that entailed flying General TN all over northern Laos in the soon-to-be armed-to-the-teeth Huey. Hank, and later Thatch, were offered positions as crew for Jim. This would necessitate some training, mostly on weapons, which would be arranged by Bill. It would also give Bill full knowledge of any and all activities the crew engaged in.

The Huey gunship would be based at Udorn on the Air America side of the field, but it would be separate from Air America. The space designated for General TN and his airline would be known as an off-limits site. If you didn't work there you didn't go there.

TN named his airline RAJAIR. It consisted of two nearly new unarmed Bell 205s and a Volpar in addition to Jim's Huey. The general had the 205s painted black with RAJAIR on each side in white. Jim convinced the general to leave the Huey painted drab green so it would not be so easily recognized and possibly become a target. The general agreed, and the Volpar remained painted its original green and white.

It was believed that the black 205s gave birth to the ensuing legend that the UN was operating the black choppers. This legend followed some of the troops home and lived on among some of the far-out survivalist communities. It was also believed that Bill was the original source of this legend, for whenever he was asked about the black choppers, he always casually responded that they were the property of the UN.

The staging and maintenance of the general's air operation was established and manned by both American and Thai crews. They were instructed to ask no questions if they wanted to stay part of what was a cushy assignment. They had decent quarters, a light work load, and very little supervision. It was a dream assignment as long as they didn't piss off General TN. The general's explosive nature was well-known around the base, and the boys had first begun to refer to him as General TNT. Later that handle morphed into Nitro. To his face, he was General T or TN, but safely behind his back, he became known to the troops as just plain Nitro.

The general's plan was very basic and backed with muscle. After all, he ran the ground army, and anyone that didn't fall into line would be dealt with severely. First, the general informed the tribal poppy growers that RAJAIR would be picking up all of the fruits of their labors. They were not to contract with anyone other than him. He, in turn, would pay them the going rate. Of course, the going rate would eventually be established by General TN.

The poppies bloomed seasonally. After blooming, the pod contained the prized sap. The seeds were gathered for planting the next crop. The pod was then lanced, allowing the sap to ooze out of it. This sticky gunk was raw opium and was then collected and shaped into softball-sized spheres that smelled like hell and were valued by their weight. This prize was the ingredient that started the process. The general established two processing factories in northern Laos.

The black RAJAIR 205s would pick up the stinking raw opium and deliver it to the two ramshackle factories for processing. After processing, the ensuing powder would be sized and wrapped in plastic. The brick-sized packages would then be sold for cash. Next, after an electronic exchange of American dollars, the processed opium—now referred to as heroin—would be delivered to a clandestine location in Thailand via the RAJAIR Volpar. Air America had no involvement whatsoever in this operation. It was a one-man show with General TN calling all the shots.

The 100 percent opium would be processed and mixed (cut) with various ingredients at the generals factories. A ball of opium that initially cost one hundred dollars would, after processing, bring the general over 1.5 million dollars.

By the time the end product reached the streets of a major city after being cut many more times, the cocaine—as it was then called—would generate over five hundred million dollars in sales. It was big business with very little up-front risk for the general. His coffers swelled.

Chapter 19

Jimbo's new gunship was outfitted with the usual rocket pods and two door-mounted M60 machine guns on either side. Thatcher and Hank received their training from an American-trained Thai military sergeant who had been assigned to the ground crew. They learned firsthand how to handle the M60s, both on the ground and in flight. Additionally, they learned how to load the pods and arm the rockets.

During their checkout flights, they off-loaded extra munitions at the various outlying posts so that they could re-arm in the field if necessary. They had no idea where General TN would ask them to go or what they would be doing, but they knew it would not be long before they became the general's principal mode of transportation.

It was during one such training flight that they overheard an emergency call they assumed came from an American military craft that was down and in trouble. Enemy ground forces had the pilot pinned down in an open field, and one of the responding Air America rescue craft had also crashed attempting to make an extraction.

On this particular day, the enemy was playing a game of cat and mouse. They were waiting in ambush for the unarmed Air America craft to come their first victim's rescue. They were determined to shoot down as many rescue craft as they possibly could.

An Air America Cessna observation plane was at altitude overhead, warning those who answered the distress signal that one Air America rescue helicopter was already down and damaged alongside the initial Huey that had gone down. It was developing into a quagmire. The jolly greens, though in route, were still some time away.

Then an alarming message cracked from the Cessna pilot, "The bastards are advancing on the downed craft. It appears we have wounded on the ground. This is bad … real bad."

As if on cue, a new voice cracked to life. "Cessna observation, this is Jimbo Zero One."

"Roger, Zero One."

"Cessna, advise all aircraft to depart the area, and you should move to a very safe altitude."

"Jimbo Zero One, do you know something I don't know?"

"Roger that, my friend. Stand by. We will be overhead in less than a minute."

"And then what, Zero One?"

"All hell is going to break loose. Repeat, all craft stay at a safe altitude. Zero One out."

The enemy knew they had to get in, take the prisoners or kill them, and get out before the "jolly green giants" arrived and raked them with machine gun fire. They saw the window, and they moved to execute their plan. Moving briskly out of the wooded cover they had been maintaining, the enemy was closing in on their prey when Jimbo's Huey made its first pass. He lit them up with a bevy of rocket fire that decimated their irregular advancing line.

Initially stunned, the enemy survivors regrouped and stared skyward in disbelief. On Jim's second pass, Huey Zero One raked the enemy survivors with M60s, and as the remaining forces retreated to the envisioned safety of the wooded area, another rocket blast leveled the remaining few. There would be no survivors to tell of what happened.

Zero One landed before the dust cleared and began to on-load the survivors.

"Wounded first!" Hank shouted as he raised his M60 to a safe position.

Jimbo's crew was mutually astonished to see General TN among those on the ground. TN helped place his wounded pilot aboard and then an Air America pilot and copilot who had attempted to rescue them.

The general quickly climbed aboard, and Jim shouted and motioned for him to get up front and to occupy the copilot seat. The general eagerly responded. He was not yet buckled in when Jim abruptly raised the Huey up and out of there.

"Zero One, nice show. Where the hell did you come from?"

"Hey there, Cessna. For the record, we were never here."

"Zero One, will we be seeing you around these parts again?"

"Roger that."

"I'd like to buy you and your crew a drink sometime."

"Got a few guys aboard that will probably beat you to that. Thanks for the assist. Will take a rain check on the drink. Over and out." Jim turned to the general. "General, would you mind taking the controls?" he asked nonchalantly.

General TN was at a loss for words. The Air America pilots always bristled when he asked to fly their choppers. "Thanks, Jim, for saving my ass. And yes, I'll take the controls."

The smile on the general's face was one of relief and pride. After all, it was his airline, and he had just survived what should have been his end. That very moment, he vowed to never forget this day. Jimbo, Thatcher, and Hank had proven to TN that they were fearless under fire, and he would repay them in his own way someday.

The wounded were not in bad shape at all. Thatcher tended to them while Hank broke out the Bud's. They had begun a practice of "having a few" on the way back to Udorn, and today would be no exception. Since the general was flying, he was not offered a cool one. He didn't seem to mind. After he took up the heading Jim provided and some ensuing silence had passed, he asked, "Jim, how long until we reach Udorn?"

"We are probably twenty minutes out, General"

The general glanced at his blue-faced Rolex and smiled once again. He had cheated death today. It was exhilarating.

***

Jimbo Zero One and crew would be involved in numerous rescues or assisted rescues in the ensuing years, many times with the general aboard. Their reputation became well-known and respected even though everyone knew that Nitro was the king pin in the dope business. No one really gave a rat's ass what he did. After all, it was a victimless crime. Additionally, Jimbo One Zero was becoming a legend in northern Laos even though not one official report had ever been filed on their activities.

Flights into and out of combat zones increased. There were a few close calls, a few holes popped into the fuselage, but nothing really serious. Jim and his crew were living on the variable edge of life with each and every flight, more so than the others, for they went looking for trouble while the others did their best to avoid it.

Monsoon season came and went. Burning season came and went. New poppies fields were planted and harvested. The never-ending cycle perpetuated as it had for hundreds of years. It seemed as though, year after year, nothing ever changed in Laos. However, change was coming.

In 1975, Jim and his crew began to notice the activity level start to wane. Bill reassured them that nothing was afoot, that they were winning the war, and that the enemy was running out of options. "Just keep doing what you are doing, and everything will be just fine" was Bill's favorite saying. The boys weren't so sure of that. Their instincts told them otherwise, but they had always trusted Bill, and Bill had always delivered.

Abruptly, at the end of an out-of-the-blue meeting one morning, Bill told Jim to take some time off for R&R. He told Jim to get his crew together and he would arrange a ride to Bangkok for a long weekend. Jim, Thatcher, and Hank needed a breather, and at the insistence of Bill and with confirmation from General TN, the three took some R&R time and flew to Bangkok. They hopped a flight with General T's Volpar, sans any heroin, and proceeded to raise holy hell. They went first class all the way, as they could well afford to.

Thanks to Bill and the CIA, the boys were contractors rather than employees. Thus, the three of them each had a private numbered retirement bank account in an Australian bank that was controlled by the CIA. As they were paid handsomely, with no tax consequences, it was impossible for them to ever spend even a small portion of their earnings. Although, on this particular four day weekend, they gave it the old college try.

"Is it time?" Hank asked.

They had pulled an all-nighter and were having breakfast at the bar.

"Afraid so, Hank," Jim replied.

"Just one more day or so," Thatcher pleaded.

Jim stretched, yawned, and looked around the room, then back to his two buddies. They were the only friends he had in the world, and it was now his responsibility to get them on the flight back to Udorn and from there, back into the war. He sat at the table, with his head cradled in his palms as he momentarily reflected on the past several years. "Where the hell do we go from here?" he asked himself rhetorically.

"What's that, Jim?" Thatcher asked, hoping it was a reprieve from their pending departure.

"What? Oh nothing Thatch … just thinking out loud. Come on. Let's get our gear, check out, and head for home."

Jeez, he thought. *Home! This is going home?* The years had taken a toll that was just becoming apparent to his exhausted state of mind. *Home. I don't have a goddamn home.*

Upon their arrival at the airport, Jim also found out he did not have a pilot. The plane was there, but the pilot was nowhere to be found. They waited around for a short fifteen minutes or so for the pilot to show up, and then they approached the flight operations desk. The English spoken was just okay, but the consensus was that the pilot had left a message for them.

"Well, just what is the message?" Jim asked impatiently.

The reply was abrupt. "You want ride home, you fly plane yourself."

"No problem. We're out of here, boys."

As Jim and his pals flew back to Udorn, they discussed their return to action. A somber mood slowly crept into their conversation. They began to verbalize what they all had been thinking lately. The war was not going well, and they had better start thinking about the future.

After a safe landing at Udorn and a short taxi to their private area, things didn't look quite right to them. They were surprised to find no one there to meet the plane. There was no ground crew and no other aircraft present on the Air America side of the Udorn runway. RAJAIR was abandoned.

They secured the plane and gathered on the tarmac.

"Well if anyone knows what the hell is happening here, it has to be Bill. Let's hustle on over to his office and find out what's going on here."

Bill's outer offices were void of any personnel. However, Bill was seated in his office at his desk with a fresh bottle of Scotch just to his right and four clean glasses standing at attention.

"Hey, boys. Just the guys I want to see. I've been expecting you for hours. How was the trip? Never mind. I know the answer. And speaking of answers, I suppose you three are here looking for some."

Hank, never very political, spoke first. "What the hell is going on?"

"Oh, so you want to cut right to the chase."

"Hank, back off a little will ya?" Thatch had his two cents worth, and then Jim followed up, "Bill, what the holy hell is going on?"

Bill slowly opened the Scotch; it was a twelve-year-old bottle. He quietly poured two fingers in each glass, including his own. After sliding theirs forward, he sat up straight in his worn out chair and offered a toast. "Boys, it's over."

"Over, Bill?"

Bill raised a silencing left hand and downed his drink with his right as he encouraged the others, with his now-outstretched hand, to follow suit. He refilled their glasses and appeared ready at last to speak. Jim couldn't help but remember that this was the way they had started out together so many years ago.

"Gentlemen, we have been ordered to shut down the entire operation. I am leaving this part of the world for parts unknown at this time." He continued, "Your fearless leader, General TN, also known around here as Nitro, has disappeared. Some think he was disposed of by his fellow countrymen, but I suspect he has fled the country for I don't know where. Nor do I care."

"Where does that leave us, Bill?" Jim asked.

All three emptied their second glass and were on the edge of their respective chairs. Their throats had gone dry.

"Well, Jim, you guys I do care about." Bill reached for the Scotch and then thought better of it. "Let's talk a little bit more with a clear mind, and then if you wish, we can drain the bottle. There's plenty more where that one came from."

Without so much as a breath, he continued. "Actually, I could use some food. Why don't you guys get some rooms at the Paradise and clean up a little. Ya stink. I'll join you for dinner."

Deja vu, Jim thought. *We have come full circle.*

"Boys, I guarantee you will not be left blowing in the wind. I have an idea that I wish to share with you. You just have to be able to think big, with a capital *B*. Trust me. We'll discuss this over dinner."

The *trust me* made Thatcher and Hank extremely nervous. As for Jim, he was intrigued. He, indeed, trusted Bill. Dinner would prove to be interesting beyond their wildest imaginations. They decided to skip the bar and proceed directly to a table instead, thus breaking a long-held tradition—a harbinger of the change that was about to come their way. Dinner became unimportant once Bill began speaking in a hushed tone. A round was ordered and delivered just as he began.

"Gentlemen, for years I have had an idea of starting my own business. I'm too tired to follow through on this idea, but I'm willing to share this info with you three in return for some financial consideration down the road, so to speak." Bill sipped his drink. "We all know that I could have gotten very rich had I elected to participate in some of the unsavory activities we have all witnessed here. But I have a certain code that I abide by and will not violate, and thus I have not profited from this war in any way, shape, or form.

"My long-term dream is to settle in Costa Rica and operate a boutique hotel. I need some financing to exercise an option I have with the elderly owner of such a hotel. My plan is to retire when I return stateside." He paused with one of his patented deep breath pauses. A couple of soft sighs broke the silence, but not a single soul spoke up. No one took the bait, so Bill went on.

"Here is what I am going to need. First, a mortgage on the hotel and second, a larger pension than I am ever going to receive from Uncle Sam."

The three amigos were bewildered. Their eyes met without blinking, and they shared a what-the-hell stare.

Thatcher, with his financial background and analytical mind spoke up first. "Bill, are you looking to us to finance your retirement? Christ, we have some dough stashed away, but it is in no way enough to help you with your dream retirement."

"Quiet down and listen, you guys. Just listen." Jim wanted the floor, for he sensed there was a lot more that needed to unfold here. "Bill, is your business idea, which you previously referred to, the root of all this financial wherewithal?"

"Exactly, Jim."

"Well then, let us get on with that part of the discussion before we spend any more time on you and your retirement haven." Jim was growing a little impatient.

Bill had led with emotion rather than common sense and thus was having a little trouble staying on track, but he gathered himself and gave them a broad brush stroke of his "plan."

"Look guys, this is how it works. Every government intelligence organization in the world operates just about the same way. They have agents scattered around the world, and they report directly back to the home office so to speak. Their information is processed to death, and most of it ends up in the goddamn shredder. The various agencies despise talking to one another. Even within our own country, the FBI and the agency withhold information from one another as a matter of policy. Do you think for one minute that Mossad or M3 really share with our agency everything they gather? Don't bother answering. They damn well do not. Now here's the crux of my idea."

Bill took a breath and a sip of his scotch and plowed ahead. "I have a list of American agents that can be trusted. They are not only aware of my idea, but they are chomping at the bit to be in on it. They in turn have their own lists of foreign agents that they trust explicitly. What I propose is that when these various agents file their field reports, they also copy a central clearing house on everything they gather. The clearing house, my brainchild, will then compare the incoming information for common threads. These innocuous threads can only be detected when the reports are overlapped. This will never happen in the ordinary course of events around the world."

"How does one make big bucks out of that?" Hank was doubtful.

"You sell the goddamn information," quipped Thatcher.

"Sell it to whom?" Jim asked.

"Now you're getting it, boys. Now you're getting it." Bill could see their light bulbs glowing bright. He was pleased with his "boys."

"Sell it to whom?" Jim persisted, and their eyes met.

"Look, you sell it to the people in charge. You sell it to the country that is about to become the recipient of a terrorist act or attack. Always sell it to the people in power, for they have the money. I can tell you that the Middle East will become a hotbed of such activity. You sew some threads together that some terrorist act is afoot in Saudi Arabia for example. Those royals will pay you a small fortune for that kind of information, and there are many other fiefdoms and kingdoms that will do likewise. They are all paranoid and flush with petrol dollars."

Bill elaborated some more and explained that they would have to set up a backroom operation capable of screening the agent's reports. They would have to have language experts aboard. Computers were something they would have to look into, etc.

"What the hell are computers?" Hank was mystified, and they ignored him.

The conversation went on and on for hours. Bill had the American agents all lined up, and they in turn had their foreign agents lined up, and Bill was ready to rock and roll because he had found the perfect guys to run the enterprise.

"Bill, it would take millions to set up such an operation. I know, for I did something similar on Wall Street years ago." Thatcher knew what he was talking about, and the others agreed.

"Another thing, Bill," Jim spoke up again. "What's in it for the agents?"

"Good question, Jim. Here's my vision. The agents end their careers with a government pension and some attaboys. What's in it for them is a potentially huge additional pension from your organization. They get a percentage of each deal that they contribute to. You set the money aside in a numbered account with an independent manager. Upon retirement from their respective agency—and only upon retirement—they will supply you with a new agent contact to replace them, and you will ensure that they begin to draw down an additional pension in the form of an untraceable tax-free annuity. We can work out the details later, but understand I am to get a percentage of everything you take in. We can also talk about that later."

"All right, all right," Jim spoke with some salivation. "Just say we are able to do all this on the scale that you envision. How the hell can this be accomplished without the millions Thatch referred to earlier?"

Jim was exasperated. The concept was unique, and he was able to grasp the uniqueness. The inside track with Bill's contacts, okay he got that. The potential earnings were possibly in the hundreds of millions of dollars, which was easy to salivate over. However, the price of entry was easily out of their reach.

Silence fell over the table. It was late, and the dining room was empty as Bill ordered another round. He had another round of information to pile onto the boys' already burdened shoulders.

"Boys, there's more." Bill flashed his signature grin, which never failed to garner attention from those that knew him, and these three knew him well. "You would have eventually found this out, but I'm going to give the news to you first. Good old Nitro never forgot about you guys saving his sorry ass that day up in the highlands. Before he disappeared from here, he asked me to tell you how much he enjoyed knowing you and fighting alongside of you."

"Come on, Bill. You're making me tear up." Hank had always had lousy timing.

"Shut up and listen, damn it." Bill frowned momentarily but recovered his grin as he sipped his scotch. "Nitro did one other thing, boys. He arranged for a deposit in a Cayman Island Bank of fifteen million American dollars to be divided into three separate accounts in each of your names. You have more than enough to launch this venture."

"Whoa, whoa, Wild Bill. Hold your horses. I'm a dead man. How the hell can I tap a bank account in the Cayman Islands? My retirement account is numbered, and I don't need a name to withdraw money. However, *five million* in an account under my name? Christ, Bill. I can't touch it. I'm dead, damn it. I'm a dead man," Jim was repeated himself out of fitful frustration. He collapsed back into his chair and left his arms dangling at his sides. He couldn't muster the energy to look at the others.

Bill surveyed all three and laughed a quiet laugh that usually meant he was getting pissed off. However, he understood Jim's concern and had anticipated this day for some time. "Listen up, you dummies. I told you long ago that I would never leave you blowing in the wind, didn't I?"

A pronounced reply was immediately proffered.

"Goddamn it, Bill. Yes, you did. I believed you then, and I believe you now." Surprisingly, the affirmation came from Hank, though it was perforated with a tone of desperation.

"Listen to me, and listen well." Bill took control of the conversation once again. "Hank and Thatch, as of today, you are both listed as killed in the line of duty. Therefore, your contracts are canceled. Sorry, boys, but there'll be no more paychecks for any of you. Jimbo, as you stated earlier, you are already dead and buried.

The others stifled the urge to turn and look at Jim. They just let the remark pass.

Bill continued, "All three of you have new identities established compliments of the agency. A complete history has been established for each of you, including birth certificates, education credentials, driver's licenses, etc. You have dual citizenship in France and Switzerland and corresponding passports. Your new names are the names under which your five million dollar accounts have been established. Your past will be invisible if you play it smart. Moreover, you will play it smart, and as a group you will launch this venture. All for one, and one for all, boys. As you know, I do not like loose ends."

The threat was not veiled. Bill wanted his retirement on his terms, and he was willing to see them become extremely wealthy in order for him to have his "humble retirement." It was to be a two-way street. The boys knew Bill could make them disappear at any time, for he was truly connected around the world.

"I'm in."

"Count me in."

They looked to Jim.

"It's unanimous," Jim said.

They touched glasses.

"Don't get too drunk tonight, boys. Meet me in my office midmorning, and we will go over the balance of the details. By the way, when you get to the Cayman Islands—and you *are* going to the Caymans—change your bank accounts to a new account and change the passwords. After that, enjoy Paris or wherever else you decide to set up your headquarters, and don't waste a lot of time doing it. Just stay in touch with me. I'll give you six months, and then I'll expect to hear from you on a regular basis."

The survival skills and the drive to win that they had perfected in Laos would serve them well as they set up their new business venture. Bill provided the initial direction, along with a good kick-start of contacts. The rest would be up to them.

Chapter 20

Thanksgiving 2001 was just a few days away. True to his word, Jim was on his way to visit his brother, Joe, and the family in northeast Florida.

When Jim had begun to trace his roots, he had his organization do a complete background check on Joe McDonnell. He was armed with a file an inch or so thick. He knew all about Maggie. He knew about their relationship with Julia, and he also knew everything there was to know about their son, Mike.

Hell, he even knew the layout of Joe's new home. He knew about Joe's twin engine plane that was housed at the St. Augustine Airport, and he even knew Joe's golf score, which was not very good. Yes, Jim had all the information on his brother, and his brother knew absolutely nothing about him after the age of twenty-four. However, Joe at least had the memory of those first twenty-four years of Jim's life, and he was the sole possessor of every memory that was associated with that time in their lives.

Jim knew he would have to be very upfront right from the beginning. He would have to look his brother in the eye and tell him that he had no memory of ever knowing him, even though he knew for a fact that they were brothers.

All of this was playing in Jim's mind as time grew closer and closer to their Thanksgiving meeting. Another bittersweet thought was also in need of addressing. Jim had approved the recruiting of Mike McDonnell into the Blue Seas organization with no knowledge of his relationship to Joe McDonnell. At the time, Jim had known nothing of Joe. Jim had also come into contact with Julia Bond in late summer of 2001 while he was in Washington, D.C. attempting to make contact with the new FBI terrorist group that was headed up by Julia and her partner, Ferp Webster.

Blue Seas had not attempted to do business with the United States because of the fractured nature of its various domestic intelligence organizations. No one shared information, and Blue Seas saw no financial opportunity for them in the United States.

Nevertheless, in June and July of 2001, Blue Seas had picked up information in their system that something big was in the works for the east coast of the United States. They could not pin down the details, but they had gleaned enough information that Jim felt obligated to make contact with the FBI, and he had set about contacting Julia and Ferp to arrange a meeting. Julia and Ferp were in charge of the newly formed anti-terrorist group within the FBI. Things never worked out. The FBI set up what Jim considered a trap to arrest him, and after some initial phone contact, he beat a hasty retreat. The FBI thought he was not plausible, and there had been no follow-up.

Meantime, Jim and his partners—against their better judgment—in 2001, had decided to test the U.S. market. They hired several new agents to establish a presence in the United States. That's when Mike, Julia, and others had come aboard the Blue Seas organization as field agents. None of the new agents had ever met Jim face-to-face.

It was during the waning days of summer, just prior to September 11, 2001, that Blue Seas had pieced together some additional intelligence threads that indicated a potential terrorist act was planned for NYC and D.C. Blue Seas had also determined that the attack would involve multiple commercial U.S. aircraft.

Conventional wisdom within Blue Seas had led them to believe that several hijackings were being planned in NYC and D.C. Jim had not believed that would be the case. He had felt it could possibly be something of a greater magnitude.

Using its channels, Blue Seas had passed the information about the pending terrorist act to the CIA. It was a backchannel move that was uncharacteristic of BSE. However, it was reported back that since the CIA was not involved in domestic activities that, though passed along through domestic U.S. channels, the warning was not taken seriously.

By this time, Jim had known Joe was his brother and that Joe had traveled from Florida to NYC for a charity book signing event on September 8. He decided to warn him in such a way that Joe would heed his warning and get the hell out of town. He had hoped to meet up with Joe under different circumstances, but he had been delaying such a meeting out of a foreboding sense that it would just not work itself out. He had a disguised fear of rejection.

On top of this load, he had also piled the weight of the recent decision by Blue Seas to completely abandon the United States as a potential source of intelligence sharing for a profit. The Blue Seas agents were to be informed that their services would no longer be required. Julia and Mike were about to join the ranks of the unemployed. Blue Seas would stick to the knitting, so to speak, and continue to operate in the Middle East and Asia.

Jim had a lot on his mind as he stepped up, stuck his head into the cockpit, and told the copilot to take a break and exchange seats with him. Jim loved taking the controls of the Falcon. Actually, the craft was flying on autopilot, but he loved to sit up front for a while on long flights, and it gave the pilots a needed break. If need be, he was certified to pilot the plane. It was a new model twin engine corporate jet that Blue Seas Enterprises had just taken delivery on.

They were en route to Florida from their home base in Paris. As he had promised in New York several months ago, Jim was going to pay a long overdue visit to his brother, Joe.

Jim sat silently staring out over the Atlantic some 30,000 feet below. He thought about the irony of how one of the frequent passengers on the old BSE jet had left behind a copy of Joe McDonnell's novel, *Hallowed Gesture*. Jim had read the novel and had felt extremely unnerved but also intrigued.

Jim had had his people at Blue Seas delve into Joe's background, and the summary report that had come back to Jim had strongly suggested that the author, Joe McDonnell, had had a brother and that Jim was very likely that brother. The brother, reportedly, had died in action in Vietnam in 1968. Blue Seas had obtained a copy of Jim's military file, and they put the pieces together. From that day forward, he began to think of himself as Jim McDonnell instead of his current persona, James Montie—a name supplied by Bill Coade years ago when they had all left Laos. Bill had arranged for Jim to keep his first name as part of his new identity, for Bill liked to refer to Jim as Jimbo.

The brotherly reunion was to take place at Joe's home in northern Florida over the Thanksgiving holiday. Jim was hopeful that through conversation, old pictures, and some old-fashioned reminiscing, he would be able to make a connection that would kick-start his blank memory back to life. Jim was counting on that happening because he had never married, and thus the only true family he ever had would never become part of his life without some breakthrough with his memory loss.

Jim returned to the main cabin and sat in one of the plush leather swivel seats. As the Falcon Jet soared at 600-plus miles per hour above the ocean, he thought some more about life.

"Christ, what a life," he murmured to himself. Then, tilting back his head, he began to dwell on the past.

The only negative since surviving the war and returning to civilian life was that fact that he had no family. However, that aside, life had been very, very, sweet for him, Hank (now John Pierre), and Thatcher (now Nathan Webster).

BSE had been one hell of an adventure that had dripped nothing but profit almost from day one. They were extremely wealthy and worldly men that kept a low profile and stayed off life's radar. Their success had allowed them to sample all the pleasures they desired, but outside their own circle, they could not muster the trust to sustain a significant relationship. They had each experienced numerous relationships that lasted but a short time.

By focusing mainly on the business, they had managed BSE into a magnificent international operation. So much so that most of the employees had no idea what the end products of their endeavors were. There was a tight-knit group of five individuals that were privy to most everything. They ran the enterprise on a day-to-day basis, and at the top sat the three musketeers.

You know, I would give it all up tomorrow if I could make a mental connection with my brother, Jim thought desperately. As the jet approached the mainland of the United States, he dozed off.

The landing at Jacksonville (JAX) was uneventful. After clearing customs, the pilots secured the plane and would spend the next couple of days playing golf while Jim went about his business. None of them had any idea that another jet, just clearing customs, had followed them across the Atlantic and that the two passengers were hot on the trail of Jim (McDonnell) Montie. In fact, they had been only minutes behind him at the rental car facility.

Jim safely motored away from the airport in his luxury rental car. He entered his destination into the onboard navigational system and headed south on I-95. He was full of anticipation, for he really had no idea what to expect. He wanted so badly for his memory to return. He was about to meet a brother he didn't remember a damn thing about other that the fact that he had written a novel that had ultimately lead them to each other.

The navigational system indicated Jim should exit on to 9A, but the exit ramp was blocked by a state police cruiser with flashing emergency lights and a bevy of glowing red flairs. Jim continued south on 95 and re-entered his destination information. Shortly, an alternative route to the east was identified, and it required him to continue South on I-95, directly through the city of Jacksonville. He relaxed and figured it would be nice to see the city for the first time and the delay would be minimal.

Jim was unaware that the two unsavory individuals that had followed him to Jacksonville were racing in the distance in hopes of catching up to him and, if the opportunity presented itself, complete their task by killing him.

Making the best out of the slight delay, Jim went back to his thoughts about the upcoming meeting with his brother, and the anticipation returned as his mind wandered back over the seemingly wasted years he had spent in Asia. But then again, he thought, without those years he would probably not have been in the enviable position he now enjoyed in life.

"Well, goddamn it," he verbalized as he sped past his exit in total oblivion to the directions from his navigation system. Composing himself, he was resigned to making a U-turn at the next exit when the onboard system suggested an alternate route that would not necessitate reversing his direction of travel. He resolved to shelve his mental wanderings and pay attention to the road. As directed, Jim exited I-95 onto Route 1 south. From there he was to travel eastward on Route 210 to Ponte Vedra. *Simple enough,* he thought.

The early fall evening in northern Florida was darker than usual due to the overcast sky and the threat of rain showers. Otherwise, it was a pleasant time of day, and Jim attempted to ignore his directional guffaws and the butterflies that flapped wildly in his stomach. He had just reached to change the music station when his cell phone rang to life. The call was unexpected, and Jim was caught off guard as he checked the caller ID and responded.

"Hello, Jim here."

"Jim, your phone is not secure, so I will be brief and to the point."

"Quinton, is this you?"

The person on the other end of the line responded affirmatively. Quinton was one member of a five-person management team at BSE. This elite team controlled all of the daily activities at Blue Seas. They were the inner circle and were privy to all matters. They answered only to the three founding partners.

"Jim, listen. John and Nathan are dead. We're convinced they were assassinated."

"We? Quinton?" There was a slight tremor in Jim's voice.

"Yes, Jim, the entire team is in on this call. We believe all three of you were targeted to be killed simultaneously. Your trip out of the country possibly saved your life. We believe you are a target and suggest that we execute our disaster plan immediately. Do we have your blessing?"

Jim was shocked into momentary silence, but then he responded. "Quickly now, tell me more about the nature of their deaths."

Quinton hesitated before responding. "They were found dead at home, with one shot each to the back of the head. The belief is that they both died around the same time."

"Execute the disaster plan immediately. I will go underground until we get to the bottom of this." When Jim issued the command, the voice tremor was gone and replaced by a take-charge tone. "Try to keep the deaths low profile. You will hear from me in due time. If I don't resurface, I trust you will carry out the plan just as we designed it. Any questions? Thought not. Good-bye." Jim immediately turned off his cell phone. It was 8:00 in the evening, and he quietly gathered his thoughts.

Okay, no more cell phone use. I don't dare rule anything out. Therefore I can't proceed to Joe's house. Someone could have followed me to JAX. Don't want to bring any of my problems to his doorstep. I need a public pay phone, and I need it pronto.

Farther on down Route 1, on the opposite side of the highway he spied a neon light. As he drove past, he observed the place as a roadside bar. He executed a U-turn at the first break in the median and backtracked. He watched for someone to follow him, and to his astonishment, a pair of headlights made the same U-turn. A coincidence? He thought not. His instincts told him danger was near, and he was unprepared to forcibly deal with it.

He nestled his car on the end of a row of Harleys. The neon sign he had observed from a distance announced the name of the establishment: The Rooster. Of all places to pick, he had picked the only biker bar within God knows how many miles. Then he thought to himself that this might not be a bad choice after all.

A group of bar patrons was gathered in front of the establishment, all with bottles of beer in hand. Some were admiring the hogs of others;

some were holding court and pointing out the various features of their own custom bikes. This activity came to a screeching halt as Jim invaded the parking area with his rental car. The bar's patrons eyeballed the invader that had just arrived in the bike-only parking area.

As Jim moved quickly from his car toward the front entrance of The Rooster, he received a not-so-warm welcome.

"Hey, mister, this area is a bike-only area. Ya got to move the car."

Jim didn't miss a stride as he responded. "Sorry folks, but I have to take a leak in a real bad way. I'll move the car as soon as I come out."

He then turned to them and quickly added. "Hey, I have a car following me, and they will probably pull in right next to me thinking that it's okay to park here. Why don't you move as a group and just block the entrance, and my friend will know enough to park elsewhere."

As if following the orders of a guru, the unwelcoming group moved as one and stood, effectively blocking the entranceway. They gave Jim a knowing smile just as the trailing car slowed to pull into the lot. Finding no place to park, the ominous car moved slowly past the establishment and would have to make two U-turns to return to the area of the bar. There was a side street alongside the bar that they missed on their first pass but not on their return. They returned, nestled in on the dark side street, and sat with their lights out and engine running.

They had to make a decision to either wait for Jim to return to his car or go in after him. They decided Jim was probably not aware that his two partners were dead and thus would have no idea of their presence. The joint had to close sometime, and Jim would have to return to his car. They would wait and nail him while he was seated behind the wheel if the timing was right. Otherwise, they would pull alongside him on the highway and blast him through the driver's side window. Either way, it would be mission accomplished before the day's end.

Meanwhile, inside Jim took a quick glance around and made sure to avoid a lot of eye contact. This was an old-fashioned, contemporary joint. It had a welcoming atmosphere, and the tattooed bartender smiled as she slapped down a circular Heineken coaster. Jim slapped down a twenty dollar bill.

"I'll have one of those." He pointed to the Heineken and followed with, "Pay phone?"

She pointed off to the right with her index finger. Then just as quickly, she served up a bottle and grasped the twenty.

"I'll need some quarters," Jim said.

She frowned, thinking her tip was going to be in change but quickly recovered when she realized he needed the change for the pay phone. Jim followed her previous pointing motion and found himself in a wide hallway that led to the restrooms. Along the wall, halfway down the hall was an old-fashioned phone booth that appeared to be a relic from an English pub.

Two quick rings brought a friendly response from Joe, and Jim's replied, "Joe, its Jim."

"Hey it's about time. Where the heck are you?"

"Listen closely. I have brought some trouble with me, and it is going to delay our reunion."

"But—" Joe's protest was cut short by Jim.

"Look, Joe. There is no time. You must listen. This situation could put both you and Maggie in danger. I cannot arrive at your house under these circumstances. Are Julia and Mike present?"

"Yes, they're right here, along with Maggie."

"Put the phone on speaker."

"Okay. You're on speaker."

"Mike and Julia, this is Jim."

Julia spoke for both of them. "Hi, Jim. We're all here, and Mike and I are anxiously waiting to meet you."

Julia and Mike had never met Jim Montie or his partners. They knew the names, but they had only met the five people that comprised the operating team that actually ran Blue Seas on a day-to-day basis. The Jim they were speaking to, as far as they knew, was a Jim McDonnell that Joe McDonnell had referred to as his long-lost brother who was coming to meet all of them for a Thanksgiving reunion.

Joe McDonnell, for his part, had never made the connection between the Blue Seas Enterprises his brother briefly referred to at their first meeting and the BSE that Julia and Mike now worked for. A stunning revelation was to follow as Jim spoke via speaker phone to the four people gathered at Joe and Maggie McDonnell's home on this quiet Florida evening.

"*Black Diamond*. I repeat, *Black Diamond*." Jim said.

Julia and Mike immediately turned to each other and nodded. Joe and Maggie looked quizzically toward each other and then to Julia and Mike, who each turned toward the speaker phone and responded immediately. "What do you need us to do?"

Maggie and Joe remained silent as the conversation continued.

"Listen, we don't have much time," Jim said. "You know me as Jim Montie. John Pierre and Nathan Webster are dead. BSE is operating under a company disaster plan. My life is in danger, thus the Black Diamond code."

As a part of the Blue Seas operations protocol, a Black Diamond code was a call to BSE field employees for immediate assistance with the prospects of a kill or be killed outcome.

"Where are you?" Mike was the first to respond.

"I'm at a bar on Route 1 in the town of Bayard."

Joe sounded in, "There's only one bar in Bayard, and I know exactly where you are."

Julia and Mike nodded to Joe.

Joe continued, "We'll be there in twenty minutes."

Jim's only response was right to the point. "No, Joe. Just Julia and Mike should come. You stay with Maggie."

Joe turned to Maggie, and she motioned with her head for him to go with Julia and Mike.

Just then, Jim spoke again. "Hustle your butts, and come armed."

Just as Jim hung up the phone, a *tap, tap* on the glass door of the phone booth startled him back to his surroundings. The booth was an oddity for a biker's bar. It was an old English style phone booth painted red with panes of glass that would be more at home in a pub than a bar. It was rumored that the owner of a pub in a nearby town had lost it in a pool game at The Rooster years ago.

Jim responded to the tap with a quick turn of his head. He expected the worst and was relieved to see two of the guys from outside wanting his attention.

"Hey, bud. What about moving the car?"

Jim, now standing toe-to-toe with the two, smiled and pulled out a one hundred dollar bill.

"Guys, I'll buy a round or two if one of you will go out there and move that damn car for me."

The offer was a no-brainer, and the men quickly accepted it by snatching the folded bill and outstretching a hand for the car keys.

"Do me one other favor," Jim said. "While you're moving and parking the car, take a look around for a car with one or two guys just sitting in it. Don't attract any attention to yourself. Just let me know."

The guy with the keys in hand gave Jim a quizzical look. "Who's the bad guy, you or them?

It was a fair question and received a quick answer. "They are." Jim's response was well received.

"They gotta be nuts to try anything in here. Just frigging nuts. I'll be right back with your keys."

The response was very nonchalant, as Jim quipped, "No. Just leave them in the ignition."

A shoulder shrug was the only response the biker offered as he headed out to move the car.

The two would-be assassins watched in amazement as the middle-aged biker casually moved Jim's rental car from the bike lot and proceeded to park it directly in front of them. The quick once-over glance the biker sent in their direction as he returned to the bar was all they needed to realize that Jim was aware of their presence and that he could be in the process of calling for reinforcements.

It was time for a change in their plans. Knowing they couldn't risk going into the bar after Jim, they immediately decided to move their car to another vantage point that was not as noticeable as their present position. They drove back onto Route 1 and headed north to the next intersection. Then, after making a quick U-turn, they pulled off the pavement onto the shoulder of Route 1 about 200 feet north of the bar. Although they were now on the opposite side of the highway, they had a good view of the front entrance while they themselves were for the most part out of sight. Two other empty vehicles, which probably belonged to some of the bar patrons, were parked farther down on the same side of the road.

Julia, Mike, and Joe arrived in Maggie's black four-door Caddy. All three were licensed to carry concealed firearms in Florida and thirty-two other states that offered mutual recognition of each other's permits. Joe had a Florida concealed carry permit. Julia and Mike's permits had been issued in Virginia. Joe always carried a small 9mm pistol in a holster in his front pants pocket. Tonight he also packed a larger capacity 9mm in a hip holster covered by his shirt. Julia and Mike both had a 9mm holstered in the small of their backs. Additionally, Joe had placed a twelve–gauge, pump-action shotgun in the trunk of the Caddy along with his old trusty .45 caliber M1911. They all had extra magazines stashed on them. As they say in military, they were locked and loaded.

Upon their arrival on the street alongside The Rooster, they took a long look around before exiting the car. It had started to rain lightly, and the bike crowd had begun to exit the bar and head for home, hoping to avoid the heavier downpour that seemed about to follow.

Joe, Julia, and Mike unconsciously aligned three abreast after exiting the car and quickly moved toward the front entrance of the bar, all the while looking around for anyone or anything that would look suspicious to them. They noticed the now-lone car parked on the opposite side of Route 1, but it was too far away to determine if it was occupied. Nevertheless, all three noticed it and shared a cautious glance.

Jim was sitting at a table as far from the front door as possible, and he was greatly relieved to see his three potential lifesavers suddenly appear in the doorway. The greetings were short as they sat down at Jim's table and positioned themselves to keep an eye on the front entrance. Jim was the first to speak.

"I had a second phone conversation with my people in Paris, and there is absolutely no doubt in my mind that I am the intended target of an assassination plot. The big unknown is why. Killing the three founders of Blue Seas does not have any material effect on the operation of the enterprise, and furthermore, we do not have any common enemies. The terrorists we uncover are never even aware of our existence. Therefore, as for motive, I haven't a single clue as to who could be behind this action. But it's for real, and I—or should I say we—need a plan to resolve this situation, and we need it fast."

"Well, we need to get the hell out of here." That was all that Joe had to offer before Mike interrupted him.

"Let's assume someone has followed you to here and that they are outside watching for an opening to get at you. It doesn't make any sense to go to Joe's house."

Julia joined in. "The house is too open, and besides, we would only endanger Maggie."

"Where in the hell do you suggest we go?" Jim asked hopefully.

"Well, if someone found you here, they could possibly find you anywhere." All eyes were on Julia as she finished her broad statement.

Then Joe chimed in. "Change the playing field. That's what we need to do. Just change the goddamn playing field." Joe sat forward in his chair as he quietly lowered his fist on the table. He had everyone's attention.

Jim was duly impressed with the quickness of his brother's assessment of the situation. "Go ahead, Joe. Finish up with your idea." Jim leaned into the table as he spoke, as did the others.

"First, we go on the offense. Let's hunt down the bastards instead of having them hunt you."

Mike joined in. "Look we still need some time to formulate a plan, and we still need to get the hell out of not only this place, but we need to get out of town to someplace where we can gain control of this situation."

Jim took in the logic of Joe and Mike's statements and decided to take charge of this discussion. "Give me a destination. Quick, the three of you come up with a destination, and then we'll work on a plan."

Julia and Joe's eyes met. She gave Joe a telltale nod of her head. Joe wasted no time at all as he quickly announced, "Scranton. We go to Scranton, PA, and we go tonight. I know the area like the back of my hand, and so does Julia. The family apartment there is in a busy area. It's fairly secure, and it's on the third floor. There's a security system with exterior cameras that can be monitored from the apartment."

Julia then added. "We could observe from street level in shifts, and if someone follows us to Scranton, it shouldn't take us long to pick up on their activity." She received a thumbs-up from all three.

Jim began to feel they might be on the right track. "Okay. Here's what I suggest we do, and feel free to join in at any time. Joe, do you still have your plane?"

"Sure, Jim, and it can be ready to fly tonight, if need be."

Jim turned to Mike and Julia. "You two will fly on my jet into Scranton. You may or may not be followed, but in either case, you two will be on your own until we get there. I believe if someone is watching me, they will stay with me. My jet will drop you in Scranton, then fly on to Teterboro, New Jersey, and wait for further instructions. You two will need to rent two cars, open up the apartment in Scranton, check out the security system, and stock up on some food and drink."

Joe hastily wrote down the security code for the apartment and just as quickly made a request, "Make sure you get some red wine, Julia."

Julia managed a dismissive shake of her head toward Joe.

Now, Jim turned his attention to Joe. "Joe, I know from a background check that Blue Seas did on you that you have a twin engine plane. I don't recall what kind of plane it is, so can you give me an idea about how long you think it would take the two of us to fly from here to Scranton?"

'Well, Jim, I have an Aerostar."

Jim interrupted him abruptly. "Aerostar! Hell, they haven't made Aerostar planes in over twenty or so years. Can you get us there in one piece?"

Joe immediately went on the offense. "Jim, this baby is completely refurbished. I've got about nine hundred Gs in it. It's pressurized to thirty-three thousand feet, and it will easily do over three hundred miles per hour. I can fly it high, and I can fly it under the radar. She's a good bird in which to make a getaway. We will not file a flight plan out of here. I'll file a plan only if the weather deteriorates and then I'll file to a bogus location. The plan can be cancelled once the weather clears. What I would like to do would be to land at a small airport outside of Scranton, then rent a car and drive into the city. It would make it all the more difficult for anyone to pick up our trail. Additionally, I would say that the flying time would be around three and a half hours or so. Sounds like a couple of drug runners making a plan, eh?"

Julia responded with a question concerning logistics. "Joe, if you figure about four hours of flying time to the Scranton area, then you'll arrive hours before you will be able to rent a car. Where are you planning to fly into?"

"I was planning to fly into Cherry Ridge, which is just outside Honesdale."

"All right, you and I visited there some time ago, but I remember exactly where it is. Why don't I meet you two there? We can stay in touch via cell phone. Our phones should be safe, and Mike can watch the apartment."

Jim, listening intently, now smiled as he spoke. "Joe, have you ever been on the run? Wait, don't answer me. That's a good plan, but we have to sweeten it up a bit. You and I can go over some additional details while we make the drive down to your airport."

It was just after 10 PM, and it was time to turn talk into action. Joe phoned the airport to arrange for his plane to be on the flight line, fully fueled. It was a twenty-four hour facility, and the shift manager—who knew Joe quite well—assured him his plane would be ready to go. Joe then went out of the bar first and pulled the Cadillac right up to the front door of The Rooster. Jim quickly entered the front passenger seat as Julia and Mike stood guard. As Jim buckled up, he noticed a twelve-gauge, pump-action shotgun tucked in between the seat and the center console.

Mike and Julia then pulled up directly behind them in Jim's rental car. They drove away from the bar in a northern direction, and they all noticed the dark car on the opposite side of Route 1 come to life. It would have to drive south for several blocks in order to make a U-turn to follow the two-car caravan as it proceeded north.

At the first intersection, Joe made a U-turn and hastily headed south on Route 1 at about seventy miles per hour. Mike and Julia continued north and made their way to the Jacksonville Airport, where they would board Jim's jet, which would deliver them to the Wilkes Barre/Scranton Airport a couple of hours later.

Meanwhile, Jim and Joe continued toward the St. Augustine airport, figuring that at best, they had a mile or so lead on the assassins.

Jim filled Joe in on the rest of his plans. "Joe, I like your idea of changing the playing field, and here's what I propose we do now. Once we get to the airport, we have to get on your plane as fast as we can. I'm willing to bet that whoever is following us will catch up to us very soon, and we have to keep one step ahead of them until we are airborne. Phone your guy at the airport. Tell him that some guys are on our tail and will probably ask him if he knows our destination. Tell your guy to act casual and tell them he overheard us mention Scranton, PA. and that's all he knows. Then ask your guy to call your cell afterward to confirm the conversation. We will then know for sure that what we suspect is true, and we will change the playing field by drawing these bastards into our turf. Or should I say your turf."

Joe quickly initiated the call and baited the trap.

Soon the Aerostar was wheels up and climbing. A turn to the northwest began what would be the merging of all the parties involved. Six people would eventually be en route to Scranton, all on a related mission, but not all would leave there alive.

Chapter 21

It was late on Wednesday evening. Tomorrow would bring Thanksgiving, but there would be no turkey or trimmings for the McDonnell party. Julia and Mike were jet-bound for the "Avoca" airport, referred to that way by most local people due to its location to the nearby town of Avoca. Avoca literally translates into *vale of tears*. There was a story behind the name, but then again, there was a story behind almost everything in the Lackawanna Valley.

Jim and Joe were twenty minutes into their flight and had just finished rehashing their thoughts on their yet-to-be developed plan of attack. They had run out of ideas, and an uncomfortable silence settled in and continued for several long minutes.

Finally, Joe spoke. "Jim, where the hell have you been for the past thirty years?"

Joe continued to stare straight ahead, out into the night sky. Silence returned for several long breaths before Jim turned toward Joe and began to speak. "Well, Joe …"

Jim began his tale as far back as he could remember, at Hong Tre. They flew along at three hundred miles per hour, and Jim spoke almost as fast as they traveled. The account really got Joe's attention when Bill Coade, Laos, Air America, and the CIA came into play. Jim explained the deception that Bill had concocted to keep him in Laos for all those years. As Joe began to loath Bill Coade, Jim finished up that era with an account of how Blue Seas Enterprises came into being. He told him how Bill had been at the heart of setting up the organization that had ultimately made Jim and his partners extremely wealthy individuals.

"You know, Joe, I'm extremely embarrassed to tell you this, but as I sit here this night talking to you, I really don't have any memory of you whatsoever. I only know what I have read from the information that my company has gathered on you."

The silence made a curtain call, and the din of the engines filled the void. Joe turned to Jim and softly in a measured sort of way and went off on a tangent.

"Mom watched television very closely when the POWs came home. She was looking for you. She stared at every face and ignored the names that were associated with them. Up to that point and time, she had never given up on you. Sadly though, when the POWs finished returning and you weren't among them, she began to rapidly fail. Too bad both Mom and Dad couldn't be with us tonight. As for your memory, screw it. You'll get it back one way or another, or damn it, we'll die trying." A tear ran down Joe's cheek as he finished his speech. Abruptly, he turned back to his outward stare.

Jim pretended not to notice as he commented, "You know, somehow I believe you're right. We could very well die trying. Let's focus on the bad guys for now and let the chips fall where they may. I'm anxious to see Scranton and our old surroundings."

"The old surroundings, as you put it, might very well be the things that help jog your memory. I have some ideas about that. Let's see what happens when we get there."

They landed, as planned, at Cherry Ridge Airport outside of Honesdale, Pennsylvania. Joe had obtained his pilot's license there years before, and while living in Scranton and writing his novel, he had visited the airport quite often. On one occasion, he had invited Julia along for the ride.

Landing outside of Scranton would make it extremely more difficult for anyone attempting to pick up on the whereabouts of Jim McDonnell. The arrival of their plane woke the resident airport manager, and he sleepily greeted them and directed them where to park the plane. Joe warmly thanked him for the service and gave him the keys to the plane in case they had to move it. Joe also asked him to fill all the tanks and told him that he would call in a few days to advise him of a departure date. It was all matter-of-fact for them as they headed to the office with a promise of a warm cup of coffee.

The manager instructed them to turn off the coffee and put out the light when they left and that the door would lock behind them. He left, informing them that he was going back to bed. Jim and Joe then waited

139

somewhat impatiently in the airport office for Julia to arrive. Joe had some friends not only at the airport; he had made contacts in the most unlikely places while spending his time writing and drinking around the area. Jim was silently impressed.

Their conversation during the three-and-a-half-hour flight from St. Augustine to Cherry Ridge had been spotty. Aside from the drive to survive, they had nothing in common other than the fact that they didn't know a damn thing about one another. At least Joe had memories of family and their childhood up until they were both in their midtwenties. Jim, on the other hand, had nothing, nada, zip.

Although Jim had filled Joe in on his past as best he could remember, he had intentionally left out some of the more gruesome details and touched mostly his years spent running BSE. He knew he would have to eventually tell Joe that he was planning to shut down the Blue Seas operation in the United States and that Julia and Mike would be out of their respective jobs. He thought that the subject would be best broached at a later time.

Julia arrived in a rental car just as the coffee finished brewing, and within minutes the three were on their way to Scranton. After clearing it with Jim, Joe informed Julia of Jim's memory loss and asked her to fill Mike in on the situation. The first stop, at Joe's suggestion, was Chick's Diner on Moosic Street. The establishment was housed in a glistening stainless steel wrap that belied its age. The diner was frequented by an eclectic group of locals and was a must-stop for many folks who had grown up in the area but now lived out of town, returning only for occasional weddings and funerals. The holidays also brought many of these expatriates back to the Lackawanna Valley. The landmark diner had been a favorite haunt of both Jim and Joe years before, especially after a night spent out on the town. Cheeseburgers with fried onions, french fries smothered in gravy, and a Coke had been their usual. However, today it would be a standard breakfast.

"Anything look familiar here?" Joe had an anxious tone.

"No, Joe, not a damn thing. Do I see a pattern emerging?"

"Well, yes and no. Well … on second thought, yes. I figured if you got back into familiar surroundings, it might help jog your memory a bit. You know, just one little memory jog could help release all the other memories that I'm convinced you must have stored in there somewhere." Joe pointed across the table at Jim's head.

"What the hell. It sure can't hurt, but you have to realize that, right now, my mind is more concerned about my ass than my memory." Jim pointed at his posterior as he spoke.

They mutually nodded and smiled at the irony of the situation.

Julia phoned Enterprise Rent-A-Car and arranged for them to deliver a second car to the diner. The plan called for Julia and Mike to go ahead and look for anything that might be a red flag before the brothers settled in at the apartment. By prior arrangement, they were not to meet up in any other public places. Julia and Mike would be there to watch their backs. They would communicate via cell phones.

After a great breakfast at the diner and the arrival of the additional rental car, they parted company. Joe filled Julia in on his itinerary, and then she drove the rental agent back to his office. She would rejoin the two brothers afterward and follow them. Jim and Joe, with Joe driving, took a short drive to the South Side with the old homestead on High Street as their first stop. They slowly motored up the steep hill and came to a halt in front of the house where they had been raised. Jim registered nothing as Joe turned left into Lavelle Court and then left again into Healey Place. They had called it an alley when they were kids, and it provided a full view of the rear of the house and the big tree that had once been home to the best tree house in the South Side, if not all of Scranton.

Jim shook his head and motioned for Joe to move on. "Nothing here, brother. Not a blessed thing."

Not one to give up easily, Joe headed up to the Connell Park baseball fields. Both brothers were charter members of the first little league teams that had played there. As they crested the O'Hara Street hilltop, Joe was wide-eyed as the fields came into view. He was immediately astonished at how many improvements had been made to the original field. Many old names began to flash through his mind. The adults that built the first field had been mostly Italian and Irish men and woman whose kids were to enjoy the fruits of their labor. He had hoped the view would have the same affect on his brother.

Grass covered diamonds, lights, outbuildings, and signage. It looked so good to Joe that even he didn't recognize the place. Obviously Jim had no chance at all of recalling the days they spent playing here on a dirt field. They quickly departed just as Joe's cell rang.

"Joe here."

"It's Mike. The apartment is clear."

"We're on our way."

"Dad, Julia told me about Jim's memory loss. Any luck with the old house or the baseball field?"

"No, Mike. I didn't even recognize it myself, let alone Jim. It's just beautiful."

"Julia mentioned you had big hopes it might jog Jim's memory." Mike spoke with disappointment in his voice.

"Yes, Mike. Damn it, I sure did. Well there's still the apartment, the downtown area, the university, the Christmas lights on the Times Tower, and last but not least, Nay Aug Park. By the way, how did you know we were at the baseball field?"

"Julia, Dad. Julia is on your tail. Good luck."

"Thanks, son." Joe rubbernecked but saw no sign of Julia.

It made Joe feel warm and fuzzy that he and Mike had patched up their relationship and that Mike and Julia had become, in Maggie's words, an "item." He made a quick stop at the Coney Island Restaurant for some Texas Wieners to go. *Thank God they are open*, Joe thought. Julia had the foresight to bring some red wine with her from Florida, for the Pennsylvania liquor stores were closed for the holiday. It was best though, because Pennsylvania prices would have staggered her. This would be the first Thanksgiving dinner at the apartment in many years.

The apartment building had been the crown jewel in their father's life. He had bought the building for a song and over a period of several years had restored the brick-and-wood framed structure on the exterior and completely remodeled the interior. The family apartment on the third floor had been two separate apartments that were converted into a single three-bedroom home for the McDonnell family after the old homestead was sold in the early 1970s.

Today, the apartment building was one of only two structures still standing on the block. The balance of the street was owned by the university, and all the old buildings had been torn down. Joe had often considered the standing offer of purchase from the university, but he could never bring himself around to actually do anything other than think about it.

They spent the rest of the evening holed up in the apartment. Joe brought out old picture albums, some slides, and even a few reels of 8mm film. But memory lane was a one-way street for Jim, and he retired that evening more frustrated than ever. Joe slept in the living room in the overstuffed arm chair, with his .45 on his lap, a 9mm in his pocket, and an empty wine glass at his side.

Early the next morning, Jim whipped up breakfast, using some staples that either Julia or Mike had stocked for them. Jim and Joe both agreed they should thank Julia for the chow. Joe mentally started planning the day as soon as he awoke. They had been only twenty minutes into their flight from St. Augustine when they had received the confirming information via cell phone that within minutes of their departure, two individuals had inquired about the destination of their flight. They figured it would take at least twenty-four hours for anyone to pinpoint their location in Scranton.

With the assumed twenty-four hour window available to them, they went about the business of trying to formulate the rest of their plan to deal with the assassins. Along the way, they visited familiar local sights with the ensuing hope of Jim regaining some memories. They started to get desperate after driving around the downtown area, which had changed somewhat, except for the Courthouse Square in the center of the city. As they walked the city campus of the university, Joe sensed some impact, but Jim was not responsive. It had all changed so much. The university had practically doubled in size.

The next planned stop was Nay Aug Park, and Joe was running out of options. Nay Aug Park was to Scranton what Central Park was to NYC. Both parks had been designed by Frederick Law Olmstead. Central Park was much better known, but Nay Aug Park contained some exceptional natural beauty within its approximately 150 acres. The waterfall at the gorge dated back to the last ice age.

Over a hundred years old, the park was a well-maintained collage of acres of lawn, gardens, and woodland. Just inside the main entrance stood an impressive multi-story limestone museum. It was named the Everheart Museum after a benefactor. The statuesque building reflected in the large Everheart Pool that welcomed visitors to the broad front steps leading up to the impressive main entrance. Two modern swimming pools were located farther into the park. They had replaced an older pool, Lake Lincoln, which at one time had been touted as the largest man-made outdoor pool in the country. The zoo, with Tillie the Elephant long gone, had been closed and remodeled. It now functioned as an educational facility. The metal bridge, which crossed a hundred feet or so above the roaring brook gorge, had long been dismantled and removed. At one time, the bridge had provided a catbird view of the gorge below and the expanded pool of water at the base of the falls.

Today, a new trail farther upstream was carried across Roaring Brook by a modern and well-designed covered bridge. On the other side of the bridge, the trail split into two branches. The right branch paralleled Roaring Brook back toward the old bridge site, the waterfall at the gorge, and the Killer 60.

The Killer 60 was a sixty-foot-high stone outcropping that overshadowed the deep pool of dark water that had been formed over the years by the roaring waterfall just above it. The Killer 60 was where people earned their stripes. Not everyone could muster the guts to step off the edge of the eight-foot-wide flat rock that cantilevered out into the space above Roaring Brook. It was so tempting to so many young guys that they came from all parts of the city to have a go at it. More walked away with rubber knees then actually took the plunge. There was no mistaking it, for the name Killer 60 was painted in white on the flat top surface of the stone.

The new route was circuitous, but nevertheless the terminus was their destination this afternoon. Joe and Jim headed up the trail to the Killer 60.

All the while, Jim questioned, "What the hell are we doing here? This makes no sense to me. We should be talking about how we are going to keep those two bastards from killing me."

"Jim, you have to trust me. We still have some time before the assassins arrive in town. I'll have a plan by then. You just have to trust me."

Trust him? For Christ's sake, I hardly know him. Jim grew impatient with the trip down memory lane as he processed his brother's *trust me* statement.

The 60 had become a recognized site, and although Jim enjoyed the beauty of the surrounding wooded area, he was perplexed as to why Joe felt this venture was worth their time.

Shortly, they arrived at the intended destination. Joe was startled to see a decklike structure covering the massive flat stone that was the Killer 60, with a safety railing all around. The uphill path terminated at a raised observation deck. They climbed the few steps to the wooden deck surface, and Joe headed directly for the railing at the edge. He stared down at the pool below and shook his head. He couldn't believe he had ever been foolish enough to jump off of this damn rock. Jim stood alongside him, observing the distant view and then the deep downward view to the swirling pool sixty feet below. The only sound was the roar of the falls below and the breeze above in the tall trees all around them. Multicolored leaves fell and floated gently into the gorge. They stood in awed silence …

"Point your toes down," Jim said.

The break in the silence startled Joe. "What's that, Jim?"

"Point your toes down. That's what you said just before we held hands and jumped."

Jim grasped Joe's left hand with his right. Their eyes met, and a tear fell. Jim moved up against the rail and bent over as if seeking a better look, but he actually was mentally visualizing the jump. As he fell, a rush of memories rapidly flashed through his mind until he stumbled back a step and took a knee to steady himself. They were still holding hands as a nervous silence overcame the white noise of the falls.

Jim, though still rattled, spoke. "Joe, the memory is spotty. There are large and little puzzle like pieces swirling in my head. I'm seeing faces with names, places with names. Mom and Dad, you as a kid, and the dog. They're all coming back. I'm on overload."

"Sit down against the railing and catch your breath. I don't know how to proceed from here. Let's just talk about whatever you feel like commenting on … or not. If you want to quietly process your thoughts, I'll just sit here and shut up until you're ready to talk."

While the McDonnell brothers revelation unfolded, Julia was parked several hundred feet from the rental car. Joe and Jim had parked in it the crushed stone parking area adjacent to the pathway that led down to the covered bridge. A third car arrived within a minute, proceeded past Julia, and parked next to the McDonnell's car. Julia slid down in her seat and went unnoticed by the two men who exited their car and walked down the steep path toward the covered bridge.

The two individuals were hyper focused on the pathway and never looked her way. They were dressed casually, and both wore dark colored windbreakers. Their shoes were street shoes, not the type one would wear for a hike in the woods. Julia observed them for a minute, and her suspicions drove her to alight her vehicle and follow them at a distance. The twosome walked down the steep trail that led to the covered bridge. They passed through the bridge, and upon exiting the far side, they hesitated and stopped at the fork in the pathway.

Julia observed the activity and did not find it suspicious at first. But then the situation changed drastically. After an exchange of words, the two men retraced their steps back through the covered bridge and stopped at the entrance. Once there, they spoke again and pulled pistols out from under their jackets and affixed silencers. It appeared to Julia that they were laying in wait for their prey to return. Julia wasted no time in beating a hasty retreat back up the path. She had to act quickly before the brothers began to retrace their steps back to the bridge.

***

Julia's voice came out of nowhere and it was forceful: "You've got to get the hell out of here, now."

When she didn't get an immediate response, she climbed the three steps up to the observation platform to find Jim and Joe sitting against the rail in silence.

"There are two of them, and they're waiting down at the covered bridge. They are armed. I'm sure they're here for you." She was looking at Jim.

Joe spoke first. "How did you get past them?"

Julia was wet from the knees down. She looked back over her shoulder toward the trail, and explained between deep breaths,   "I ran through the woods on the other side and crossed the stream just above the falls. I knew you two had to be up here somewhere."

"Then we will go back the same way that you came," Jim said. He was on his feet and past Julia in a flash. He paused and looking back. "Well, are you two coming?"

Julia and Joe bolted. Julia took the lead and showed them her previous route. They backtracked to the parking lot, where they had left their cars. The would-be perps' car was parked next to theirs. Julia departed to the far end of the lot to retrieve her car and take up a protective position. No other cars or people were in the area. It was not a good place to be. Joe took the wheel.

A quick look revealed that the keys were in the ignition of the lone other vehicle. Jim immediately hopped into the car, started the engine, and put it into drive. With a little boost on the accelerator, Jim exited the vehicle quickly. The car began to roll gently off the parking area and down a leaf-covered grassy hillside. It gradually gained momentum until it dropped over a steep embankment and into the wooded tree line.

"That should slow the bastards down." Jim was completely composed as he hopped into the seat next to Joe. "Should we just go down to the bridge and take them out?" he asked.

Joe thought over Jim's suggestion and quickly dismissed it. They were driving out of the parking lot when Joe next spoke. Julia was sitting in her car, smiling at the antics of Jim. She decided not to wait for the assumed assassins to return and followed her guys toward the park exit.

Joe glanced at Jim and addressed his previous question rather abruptly. "You know Jim, the last thing we need is a shootout at the OK Corral. Whoever is behind this would just send someone else. I know your mind must be reeling right now with the past coming back to you and also the added burden of the death of your two partners. Nevertheless, you need to focus on just who might be behind these assassins. Someone has to have hired them. Think, damn it. Think about who that person or persons might be."

Joe abruptly turned right onto a narrow blacktopped roadway. He had spotted a directional marker that indicated the Brooks Mine was ahead. Following the worn roadway for a few hundred yards led them to the mine. The mine was an old cavelike exhibit dug into the side of a natural hillside. The entrance was barred to the public these days, but one could look into the thirty- or forty-foot-deep cavern, and with a little imagination, one could visualize what an early coal mine might have looked like.

Joe stopped in front of the mine entrance and just stared at it. His mental wheels churned. He sat there, motionless, except for a faint nodding of his head.

"Joe, this is neither the time nor place for sightseeing. Let's get the hell out of here," Jim insisted.

He turned toward Jim and smiled. It was a smile of satisfaction. He at last had a plan for dealing with the two assassins that would soon be back on their trail. However, the only way the bad guys could have found Joe and Jim was by staking out the apartment area. He assumed that was how they were able to follow them up to Nay Aug Park. He called Mike to bring him up to speed, but Mike had already talked with Julia. Mike was on his own stakeout back at the apartment building. They were all surprised at how fast their trail had been picked up.

"Let's go and get a drink. Those assholes will probably end up staking out the apartment building again, which is probably how they found us to begin with. Also, that tells me that the apartment area is too busy for them to make their move."

Jim was somewhat perplexed. "How or where did you learn to think like this?" he asked.

Another smile preceded Joe's reply. "Jim ... I'm a frigging fiction writer. I think like this all the time. Why do you think I drink so much? I have so many rapid random thoughts racing around in my head that if I didn't somehow slow them down, they would speed up until they smashed an atom. Furthermore, speaking of drinking, we're on our way to Malarkie's.

I need to call in some favors. In addition, tomorrow we are going to invite the assassin bastards into our parlor."

Jim now felt the need for a drink as he gently caressed the 9mm Beretta tucked into his waistband. He could not wait to hear just what the hell his brother was creating in his fictional mind. It had better be good, for the OK Corral remark still had him slightly pissed off.

Chapter 22

Malarkey's had been a notable old-fashioned watering hole at one time. It had been rebuilt several years ago on a new site after a totally destructive fire had completely leveled the old place. The new place was a dream come true for its owner, none other than Johnny Kelly.

The bar area had retained the old-time barroom atmosphere. Oak booths surrounded the perimeter, and there were no windows. The booth seat backs were high and offered a bit of privacy. Square tables sat in the middle of the barroom, and a beautiful dark wood back bar finished off the room. The back bar was magnificently stocked with elixirs of every size, shape, color, and taste imaginable. In addition, the main floor wine cellar was the envy of the many pseudo connoisseurs that were randomly chosen for a holy tour. The back bar was fronted by a decorative fifty-foot-long dark oak bar and a lineup of swivel bar stools with sturdy backrests. The only thing missing were seat belts. The lighting was not too bright and not too dark. In Johnny's words, it was "just right."

The clientele was a mixture of young and old, depending upon the day or evening of the week. The lawyers, politicians, construction workers, college students, and an occasional biker were all part of the mixture. The food was excellent, and the place was clean from top to bottom. The Kellys ran a first-class joint. Johnny's three sons ran the place, and they ran a tight ship. What Johnny did outside the confines of his business was his business and his alone.

Johnny Kelly was seldom behind the bar these days; he left that task to his boys. He was a greeter, a real glad-hander, and he loved the role. He was around most afternoons and left the evening rush to his boys, except for Friday and Saturday nights.

Jim agreed that there was not much chance of anyone in the tavern recognizing him. They parked their car in the rear parking lot at Malarkey's, and Joe proceeded to detail his plan to Jim between phones calls to Mike and Julia. At first blush, all three cohorts expressed astonishment. Their comments varied slightly:

"Have you lost your mind?"

"You've got to be freaking nuts."

"I can't believe you're serious."

Joe challenged them to come up with a better idea, but none of them had one. Although still harboring doubt, they agreed to go with Joe's plan. As the two brothers left their car and headed toward Malarkey's rear entrance, Joe schemed a little more.

"I'll introduce you as my cousin from New Jersey. There's not much sense in complicating things at this juncture. Besides, I need a bit of time to put my scheme together, and we just don't have the luxury to delay our planning while we explain how the hell you are back among the living."

Johnny Kelly almost came out of his shoes when he saw Joe McDonnell enter his joint. "Jesus Christ, it's the devil himself."

Johnny had no idea how close he had called it. Joe introduced Jim as planned. Johnny didn't buy any of it. He couldn't quite place the guy Joe introduced as his cousin, but he knew he had seen him before, and it sure as hell wasn't in Jersey. Johnny kept his suspicions to himself and played along. They ordered a round at the bar, and then Joe nodded to Johnny that he needed to see him alone. The three of them walked the length of the bar and abruptly stopped at the end. Johnny suggested Jim take a stool while he and Joe talked business. In fact, Johnny actually pulled out a stool on the elbow of the bar and offered it to Jim. Jim figured it was a good spot to observe both the front and rear entrances and gladly accepted Johnny's hospitality. He sat quietly and took inventory of the various bar patrons.

He didn't know them by name or recognize them for that matter, but the McGee sisters were seated at the other end of the bar and had gone unnoticed by both he and Joe as they entered and greeted Johnny. Helen and Christine, both in their forties, looked quite a bit younger and were dressed very fashionably. They were graduates of "The Prep" and had obtained their undergraduate and graduate degrees from Marywood University in Scranton. No one knew what their family business was, but the girls were loaded. After graduation, they had both moved to NYC and purchased a co-op on Park Avenue. They arrived in Scranton every Thanksgiving holiday, where they enjoyed Thanksgiving dinner with a cousin. The Friday after the holiday, they always spent the afternoon at Malarkey's in hopes of running into other out of towners.

Marty, another local product who lived and prospered in NYC, looked after the folks that managed the girl's substantial trust funds. Marty was an extremely well-to-do investment banker, and he never missed meeting with the sisters at Malarkey's. This social gathering took place like clockwork every year. The trio had a tendency to get a little loud after a few drinks, but the volume was sometimes necessary on a Friday afternoon at Malarkey's. The next day the sisters, usually a little under the weather, would fly to West Palm Beach and remain there for the winter months. Marty would stay in the "friendly city" and visit family members. Most years, the sisters would return for a few days in March to celebrate the St. Patrick's Day parade, and the gathering would repeat at Malarkey's with many more friends.

At the middle of the bar sat two drinking buddies that looked to be in their early seventies. They were both WWII vets, now single and each living off of a monthly disability check. Some months they ran out of drinking money before they ran out of days of the month. Johnny always carried them on the books during those few days and the vets always came up with the dough on the first of the month. However, these two grizzled old-timers had their pride. When the need arose for them to go on the book, they each delivered their hard-won war medals, still contained in worn velvet covered protective cases, as collateral. Today was one such day, and Jim was able to observe the now-open cases that contained two Purple Hearts, a Silver Star, and a Bronze Star. Jonny's son Bobby was working the bar that afternoon. He quietly closed the cases and placed them in a drawer in the back bar. The two buddies were on the book and good to go.

Then it happened, just as everyone in the bar had expected *it* to happen. For *it* happened every day of the week, Monday through Friday, smack dab in the middle of the afternoon. Today would offer a little more interest for those in attendance as a result of the stranger occupying the barstool at the far end on the bar.

In walked Judy Lincoln. The well-recognized grand dame of Malarkey's came to the bar daily for an order of coconut shrimp and three or so glasses of red wine. Coconut shrimp was not on the menu, for there was never a request for it other than from "herself." Johnny arranged for his boys to happily oblige her, and the standing order was always served shortly after her arrival. Judy was a welcome sight and loved by all the regulars.

Each afternoon her husband, Ed—a retired school teacher—would drop her off at Malarkey's, run his errands or shop at Brunetti's, later join her for a quick drink, and then drive her home. She was no longer allowed to drive, and it had nothing to do with her age. Judy Lincoln sashayed her way past the McGee girls, proffering an air kiss and a ladylike wave of hello toward Marty and the others at the bar. All heads turned as she made a beeline for the far corner of the bar where Jim had been sitting and observing.

The five-foot-six, 125 pound dynamo walked right up to Jim, and with a big, warm smile and a light double tap on his shoulder, she made a very ladylike utterance that was heard by all.

"That's *my stool* you're sitting on, buster."

Jim sensed all eyes upon him as the bar's patrons anxiously awaited his response. Johnny had alerted Joe the minute Judy entered the place, and they also spied in Jim's direction from their booth. Johnny whispered to Joe, "If he doesn't move soon, all hell is going to break loose in here."

Well, Jim did one thing right and one thing wrong. First, he did the right thing and moved from her bar stool. But he did the wrong thing and only moved one stool to his immediate right.

Bobby, the bartender, arrived and placed a glass of her usual red wine on a coaster directly in front of her. She immediately downed about half of it. Then, with no hesitation, she turned to Jim. "So, you're new here?"

"Well, yes I am."

"I just knew it. Everyone saves this stool for me."

Jim realized Johnny had intentionally placed him on that particular stool.

"This has been my stool for years." She finished her glass of wine and was immediately served another, along with her plate of coconut shrimp. She loved her coconut shrimp.

Jim figured that with the arrival of her shrimp, he would quietly get up and leave that area of the bar to her and her alone, but she was having none of that as she placed her right hand on his left forearm and continued.

"You know, young man, I also won the Saint Augustine Beach, Florida, annual coconut shrimp eating contest two years in a row."

Jim, sensing there would be no end to this one-way conversation, added some of his own, "What happened the third year?

Before Judy could answer, Helen McGee descended on the odd couple from her end of the bar, with outstretched arms and a warm smile. As Helen hugged Judy, she flashed a Cheshire grin at Jim. Jim immediately sensed it was time to take his leave as the two ladies proceeded to ignore him and chat up a storm.

Jim abruptly stood, smiled a knowing smile, and walked away. He started toward the other end of the bar to get as far away from that woman as possible when he spotted the other Magee sister and Marty at the other end of the bar. Most of the stools were occupied by the afternoon crowd, which was rapidly growing in size. Stopping dead in his tracks, he spied an empty stool next to the two old vets and decided he would rather trade war stories than endure any more of the shrimp lady or fall prey to the two characters at the opposite end of the bar.

Bobby followed Jim to his new perch and with a big smile. He asked if Jim would like a drink.

"Yes, I would." Jim smiled. He had been set up by Johnny, and he knew it. *Her stool indeed,* he thought.

"Give me a Scotch on the rocks, and make it a double. Single malt would be nice if you have any. Also, see if these two men will have another draught."

"Boys, the gentleman would like to buy you a drink."

"We'll have what he's having," said one of them.

The other responded while pointing to the back bar, "The single malt is right up there on the third shelf to your right."

So he bought the boys a drink, dropped his chin onto his chest, and smiled. He'd been had. The vets were laughing with him, along with most of the bar patrons. Yeah! He had been had, and he loved it. Jim slapped his Amex card on the bar and bought a round for the house. It provided some much-needed levity.

Not much made Johnny Kelly twitch but Joe's request sat him up straight. "You want what, and you want it tonight?"

"Johnny, I know you can deliver if you want to. I need you to want to do this for me. It's a matter of life and death."

"You staying over at your apartment?"

"Yeah, John."

"Okay. Put your car in the garages closest to the side entrance door. By the way, what are you driving?"

"Gray Buick."

"Okay. Leave the trunk ajar, and leave the side passage door to the garage unlocked. I don't know exactly what you'll get right now, but I guarantee you it will be enough to blow up a good-sized structure. Do you need any weapons?"

"No. However, I can't stress enough how important it is that I really blow the roof off of a place. A place, which I cannot tell you about, but I need to completely destroy it."

"Christ, you don't want much, do ya? Anyway, I really don't want to know what you and your, ahem, cousin are up to."

They shook hands and exchanged hugs. Then Johnny went back to the bar as Joe continued to make a few phone calls. In the meantime, Johnny quietly speed dialed his cell phone. The plan was now afoot. There would be no turning back.

Upon leaving Malarkie's, Joe and Jim both felt a little bit better about Joe's plan. The drive back to the apartment building was short. Jim chatted endlessly as Joe happily drove and just listened. It felt so good to finally have his brother back, and Joe was determined to pull out all stops to keep him alive. Unlike Vietnam, this time he was in a position to influence the outcome, and by God, he wasn't going to fail.

After stashing the car in the garage and receiving an all-clear phone call from Mike, they cautiously walked to the rear entrance of the apartment building and were soon safely inside their apartment on the third floor.

As long as they stayed away from the windows, they would be relatively safe. The street below was always busy with student traffic from the nearby university. Julia and Mike were out there somewhere, and the infrared video cameras were almost impossible to miss seeing. No one that didn't want to be seen would dare venture into the building.

Chapter 23

Friday night came and went slowly. Joe and Jim were full of anticipation. They passed the time reviewing the same old photos that had had no meaning for Jim the day before. They catnapped and rose early. The day wore on. Finally, at exactly 3:30 PM, they briskly exited the building and headed for the garage. Once inside, Joe opened the trunk and removed a red nylon backpack.

He handed it to Jim and said, "I know the way, so I'll drive. Take a look in the bag, and let's see what kind of goodies we have."

"Well, let's see. We have ... Christ, Joe. We have two Claymore mines and ten sticks of dynamite with fuses. Where in the hell would your contact get Claymore mines?

"Oh hell, Jim. They used to manufacture Claymores right here in Scranton at the old Consolidated Molded Products plant."

"The CMP plant back in South Side?"

"That's it. I'm surprised you remember."

Jim didn't respond. He examined one of the Claymore mines and began to read aloud, "Front toward enemy."

Joe turned toward Jim as they backed out of the garage and casually commented, "We used them all the time in Vietnam. I know exactly what I'm doing when it comes to using those beauties. The fine print always faces the enemy, but they never get to read it."

Jim was quick to respond. "Not a problem, general. I think the hardest part of your planning is now behind us. It's just a matter of execution now." He thought long about the irony of his use of the word execution.

It was about a ten-mile drive to their destination. They arrived at McDade Park just before 4 PM. The last ride into the underground coal mine was scheduled for 4 PM. Mike and Julia were nowhere to be seen, but they were nearby.

The tourist ride consisted of an electric engine with several open seating cars connected behind it. The seating was two abreast, and there was room for about thirty passengers. Mike had previously purchased all of the tickets for the last ride of the day, and they were in "call waiting" for Jim and Joe to pick them up.

Joe and Jim signed the visitors' log, as requested. Joe listed Ponte Vedra, Florida, as his address, and Jim Montie listed Paris, France, as his place of residence. They then picked up all but two of their tickets and proceeded to the ride. They told the ticket lady that they didn't need the two extra tickets and that she could tell the next two tourists that the tickets were on the house. The lady smiled and gladly retook possession of the tickets.

"Boy, this will sure make somebody's day," she commented.

Frank, the ride operator and tour guide, had been contacted by phone and confirmed in person by Mike and Julia. He was halfway in on the plan but only halfway. He never would have gone along with such a scheme in his mine if he had any inkling of the magnitude of the dastardly deed they had planned for that afternoon.

While Jim and Joe stood milling about the tour loading platform, the two strangers suddenly appeared. Sizing up the opportunity and paying no attention to the backpack draped on Joe's shoulder, they immediately went inside to arrange passage on the tour train. They were amused when informed there would be no charge for the two tickets, and as requested, they respectfully signed the visitor's log, Mr. Smith and Mr. Wesson, parts unknown. They then positioned themselves outside near the tour train and waited for the operator to signal all aboard. They could not believe their luck. Fate had served up the two targets on a platter. They would soon be headed home.

Although, there were only four of them in queue, Frank spoke loudly as if addressing a large crowd. "Ladies and gentlemen, we are expecting a small school bus of children." Frank then motioned to Jim and Joe. "Will you gentlemen sit up front in the first row?" Then Frank motioned towards the distant assassins.

"Would you gentlemen please occupy the rear seat? We will place the kids in the middle as soon as they arrive."

The assassins were perplexed. They hadn't counted on kids. However, they were soon elated when Frank impatiently stated that since the bus hadn't arrived as of yet, they would begin the tour immediately for the convenience of those people aboard and he would run an additional tour when the kids arrived.

Joe's and Jim's eyes met. They exchanged a slight nod. So far so good.

The ride down the steep slope into the mine was slow, and the riders rocked slightly to-and-fro. The odd couple up front could feel the steely presence of the menacing duo riding fifteen rows to behind them. Joe and Jim quietly prayed the boys in the rear would not jump the gun, so to speak, and pop them as they entered the bowels of the mine. It was damp but well-lit as the shuttle reached the floor of the mine and came to a smooth halt.

Joe and Jim immediately left their front seat and moved past Frank into the mine. That was Frank's signal, and he performed flawlessly.

"Gentlemen, I've just been radioed that the school bus has arrived, and I need to go back up and get the kids. You can remain here and wait the few minutes it will take me to return, or you can ride back up with me." The two would-be assassins in the rear voiced that they would prefer to just wait. They immediately exited their seats. And with that segway, Frank abruptly started backing his conveyance up the slope toward daylight.

Joe and Jim were already out of sight in the mine tunnel when the assassins drew their silencer-outfitted pistols and proceeded toward their prey. It didn't take them long to make contact.

As Smith and Wesson rounded the first corner to their left, they were immediately hit by the explosion. They never saw the fine print on the front of the Claymores. Seven hundred steel balls were suspended in a hard plastic like substance in the front of each Claymore. Each steel ball was about the size of a .22 caliber projectile. The balls were backed by an explosive charge of C4. When the dark green plastic casings exploded, 1400 kisses of death greeted the two unsuspecting thugs. They went down, bloodied. Their free tickets had been punched, and it had cost them their lives.

Frank heard the explosion from above as he sat at the controls of his ride. He was transfixed for several long minutes. As part of the plan, he was to wait above ground for a call to his cell phone, which would be the signal for him to return to the mine. He wasn't in on the next part of the plan, and just as he began to regain his composure, a second explosion took place. The ground beneath his feet rattled. He had totally not expected this, and he froze again in horror. No phone call came, and he thought the magnitude of the second explosion must have been from methane gas. No way was he going to go back down there. He was in the process of dialing 911 to report the explosion when a volcanic rush of dust billowed out of the bowels of the mine and fouled the surrounding air. The few remaining tourists scattered for cover.

After the first explosion, Joe and Jim had dragged the two dead men farther into the mine. They had retrieved the men's pistols and stripped them of their identities. They then set the fuse for the dynamite and ran like hell deeper into the mine.

As fate would have it, Joe had toured the mine while he had sojourned in Scranton while writing his first novel. He had struck up a friendship with Frank and had become fascinated with the mine. He had actually toured it several times. It had been an actual working mine a generation ago, and it had been resurrected and outfitted as a tourist attraction. It was very authentic, with actual lifelike characters positioned at key locations along the circular path of the tour.

Joe had learned from Frank that there was a tunnel leading from the mine that followed a long-ago mined vein of coal. Someone could walk for miles through the opening and some offshoots. It was guarded by a jailhouse type door that was secured by a lock and chain. Additionally, less than a half mile or so into said tunnel was an air vent that opened into a cave on the side of a nearby hillside referred to as "The Patch." Frank and Joe had actually walked the short distance to the air shaft once.

After removing the prearranged opened lock and chain from the barlike gate, Joe and Jim were safely inside the nonpublic tunnel and away from the dust and grit of the second explosion. They replaced the chain and locked it, knowing full well that a search of the mine would ensue. With flashlights in hand and the help of Joe's memory of his past foray, they headed for the air shaft. Aboveground, waiting by the cave opening were Julia and Mike.

Jim and Joe welcomed the fresh air and the greeting that followed when they emerged from the hillside opening. They dusted themselves off and acknowledged their warm welcome.

"Damn, Dad, we heard the explosion from here. We were not so sure that you two were going to make it out." Mike called.

"No, we're good. We're really good. Now, get us up to Cherry Ridge, and then you two head back to Ponte Vedra. Call the car rental company and have them pick up the rental car at the mine. The keys are under the floor mat."

The forty-minute ride to the airport afforded a recap of the incident at the mine. During the drive, Jim thought back to his conversation with Joe on their plane ride up to Scranton. He determined that there was only one person he could turn to that could possibly shed some light on the assassinations. He verbalized his thoughts, and they agreed that Bill Coade was an important missing piece in this puzzle. Jim and Joe planned on paying Bill Coade an extremely businesslike visit.

They rightfully assumed that, for now, the news reports of the men missing and presumed dead due to the explosion at the mine would stave off any further attempts on Jim's life. They figured it would take days for the local authorities to organize any type of recovery effort at the mine, and eventually they would only find small body parts scattered under the rubble.

Meanwhile, the local news would pick up the victims names from the visitors log at the mine. Frank would later state that the Smith and Wesson names on the visitor's log were probably a prank and reported that only two riders had entered the mine and that he himself had been lucky to have escaped with his life. His silence endures to this day. This type of story would certainly be picked up by the wire services, and the local TV affiliates would probably get their fifteen minutes of national exposure. Yeah! It had been one hell of a plan, and they had pulled it off in spades.

"Mike, when you get back to the house, please tell Maggie we're sorry about missing Thanksgiving and that we have another trip to make and then we'll be back home."

"Where to now?"

"Costa Rica, son ... Costa Rica. Tell your mother not to worry. Oh, and one other thing, tell her the news about our deaths is greatly exaggerated."

"Easy thing for you to say, Dad. You should give her a call. She is going to be really pissed at you."

"All right, all right. I'll phone her. See ya. Much thanks to both of you for all your help."

Jim joined in the praise. "Julia and Mike, a special thanks from me."

A mutual, "Thanks, boss" and a smile was all they could muster for Jim. Joe, however, received well-deserved smart-ass glances from both Julia and Mike as Julia spoke her mind.

"This was the most unbelievable stunt I have ever partaken in. No one would ever believe me if I told them what went down here today. In fact, if I wasn't part of it, I would say no way. No way could anyone ever pull off something as farfetched as this."

"Julia, you were here, and it did happen just as I planned it," Joe retorted. "And yes, no one would ever believe you. But you know what, it might make for a good story someday."

Chapter 24

All was quiet on their western heading, except for the smooth hum of the twin engines on the Aerostar. Jim pondered their next move, for they were now operating in his domain. They had decided to not risk flying the Falcon Jet to Costa Rica because it was too big to land at the hotel airstrip. The Falcon would return to Avoca and ferry Julia and Mike back to Florida, where it would remain until further notice from Jim. The reunited brothers, flying the Aerostar, would follow an air route that would take them to Fort Lauderdale, Florida, where they would refuel and spend Saturday night. On Sunday morning, they would fly westward toward Cancun, Mexico, very careful to stay North of Cuban airspace.

Near Cancun, they would navigate southeast into the West Caribbean, careful to avoid Mexican, Honduran, and Nicaraguan airspace. Once past Islas Del Maiz, which was just north of Costa Rica, they would contact the San Jose airport in Costa Rica for permission to land. The non-stop flight from Miami would give them almost four hours to talk and plan. The thought of being over water for that period of time had Joe a little unsettled. He was not used to being so out of touch with land. Jim, on the other hand, had flown into Costa Rica on several occasions in the past. He had sometimes arrived covertly and other times for simple pleasure. Such visits always culminated with a stop at Bill Coade's hotel. Although this time the visit would be unannounced.

The conversation on this leg of the trip was upbeat. They tested each other's memories of boyhood things of no particular consequence. They covered baseball and came to the consensus that Jim had indeed been the better ballplayer. Joe was the faster runner, but Jim could run farther. It was sort of a turtle and a hare conversation.

Landmarks were another topic. Scranton Lake and the endless jogging brought a laugh. Dad would never let them have the family car to drive up to the lake for a jog. His position was that if they wanted to get into shape, they should walk up to the lake, do their jogging, and then walk back to the house. The fact that the lake was four miles from the house had no bearing on Dad's position. They both agreed that they had been in the best shapes of their lives in those years.

Scranton Lake led to a discussion of Ore Mine Spring, Number 5 Dam, Meadow Creek, and the Crusher. The Crusher was a nude swimming hole that the boys and their friends had frequented quite often in the summer months. The cry "girls on the trail" had prompted everyone to jump into the water and remain there until the intruders passed. Later on, some of the guys defied tradition and remained out of the water as the girls passed on the trail. There had been a noticeable increase in female traffic on the path that summer. Their conversation continued in that vein. There would be plenty of time on the flight back home for more serious matters.

They stayed at San Jose only for as long as it took them to clear customs, freshen up, and refuel. With the wheels up, they then headed northwest toward the Nicoya Peninsula, which was home to Bill Coade's resort hotel. Jim had been there on several occasions over the years. Bill usually arranged for a small single engine Cessna 182 to meet Jim at San Jose and fly him directly to a two-thousand-foot airstrip near the hotel that Bill had built just for that purpose. This time, though, Jim was determined to arrive unannounced.

Two subjects were burning deep inside of him. First was the death of his two partners. He was hopeful Bill could shed some light on the subject. He didn't for a moment think Bill was in any way connected to the killings, but Bill had a way of knowing things. The question was, would he share what he knew?

The second burr under Jim's saddle was his past. That SOB Bill had to have known Jim's true background while he was in Laos all those years ago. He was determined to find out why Bill had so blatantly deceived him.

"Can this baby get in and out of a two-thousand-foot runway?" Jim asked, though he already knew the answer.

"It depends, Jim." Joe mentally referred to variables such as if it was a grass, dirt, or paved runway. Additionally, the temperature, wind direction, altitude of the field, and weight of the plane at the time had to be taken into consideration.

Jim had known all of that and again asked his question. "Can the damn thing get in and get out of a two-thousand-foot paved runway?"

"Sure, Jim, why do you ask?" They were now playing.

"No reason. Just wondering," he continued. "Take her down to about twenty-five hundred feet or so and hold this heading for ten or so minutes, and we will be there.

"Aye, Captain." Joe smiled first and lost their game.

As they taxied up to the lone Cessna peeking out of a T-Hanger, a guide appeared out of nowhere and, with hand and arm gestures, directed them to an out-of-the-way spot on the tarmac.

They exited the plane and were met and greeted warmly.

"We were not expecting anyone until later today. Are you staying with us?" He introduced himself in perfect English as Jerome.

Jim spoke up. "Well, Jerry, I've met you before."

"Mr. Montie, isn't it?"

Joe turned and smiled. He just couldn't get used to Jim being referred to by a name other than McDonnell.

"Ah, yes. I'm flattered that you remember me. This fellow is my much older brother, Joe." A handshake ensued as Jim continued and directed his monologue toward Joe and Jerry. "Jerry, along with Jon—whom we will see shortly—are the two people that actually run the resort. Jerry, how long have you been associated with Bill?"

"Many years, Mr. Jim ... many years. Mr. Bill and I go back a long way, and Mr. Bill would not appreciate your kind words to me. He's the master of the house."

"All right, Jerry. He runs the place." They all laughed, and Jim and Joe accepted Jerome's offer of a ride to the hotel.

Once aboard the Jeep, Jim inquired about Bill and was cheerfully informed that indeed Mr. Bill was present and accounted for and probably readily available. Jerry knew from past experience that Mr. Bill loved to sit and drink up a fury whenever old friends visited. He still loved his scotch.

Jon greeted them from behind the front desk of the hotel. It was a long story, but Jon had once been named Juan. At one time, he had been a shoe shine boy in the lobby of the hotel. Bill had unofficially adopted him when he purchased the old place, and they now had a father-son relationship. Bill had Jon educated abroad, and he now unofficially ran the family business along with Jerry. Bill had always referred to Juan as John, and it stuck with a slight change in spelling.

The hotel had thirty rooms spread over several acres of oceanfront property. Twenty rooms were in the one-story main building, and ten others were free-standing villas. After a total renovation project in the late '70s and every ten years since, the resort had every possible bell and whistle a person could desire. Bill's dream had become a reality with a five-star rating, and he lived a five-star life. He lived in villa 30, which had an ocean view on three sides. It was located about one hundred yards or so from the main building.

It was midafternoon on a balmy day. Late November in Costa Rica was delightful. Jon informed Jim and Joe that Bill had gone on a bit of a bender and had been out of sight in his villa for two days now. He said their visit would be good medicine for Bill. After a short walk and a quick knock on the door, Jim and Joe took in the view as they waited for Bill to respond.

"Think he's out and about?" Joe asked.

"It's mid-day. He probably fell asleep after drinking his lunch." Jim knew him well.

Impatiently, Jim opened the door and called for Bill. There was no response. Jim entered and called out once more. Bill was there all right. His head was down on his desk, with a single bullet in the back of his head. Bill Coade was down for the count. Jim felt his neck for a pulse. He turned and looked at Joe. His eyes were as empty as his heart. This was a bewildering end to a long-time friendship. His eyes welled as he turned to Joe.

"He's a goner. I'd bet he's been dead for at least twelve or more hours. We better get the hell out of here. Let's go back to the main lobby and inform Jon. This is going to crush the guy." Jim was visibly shaken himself.

Joe had just half entered the room and froze in place. He had turned around to leave when Jim called out, "Wait a minute."

Jim leaned over Bill and delicately slid a half folded newspaper out from under Bill's left elbow. The newspaper showed a picture with a caption and an expansive article in Spanish. The picture had been circled several times with a black felt-tip pen, which lay uncapped on the desk. Written above the circled picture was the word *NITRO*. After all these damn years, Nitro had resurfaced with a vengeance, and Jim immediately began to put two and two together. That bastard was behind all the assassinations. He was eliminating anyone that could possibly finger him, and three out of four were now dead.

Chapter 25

He arrived as quietly as he had left Laos. First to Mexico with every forged document imaginable. His new name was now Phuy Phouma, and he asked that he just be called Father. General TN, a.k.a. Nitro, was now posing as a Catholic priest. His story was that he had come from an extremely wealthy family that had been wiped out during the war, causing him to flee for his life. He had a vision that brought him to Central America. He was going to use his family's wealth, which was now his, to set up a series of orphanages throughout Guatemala, Honduras, and Nicaragua.

The "Father" was well received and given carte blanche by the religious hierarchy in each of these countries. He went about his work with quiet devotion and financially greased any religious palm that needed greased. He had successfully disappeared for all intents and purposes.

The string of boys-only orphanages was well-run, and the Father made regular visits to his boys. The pervert always took select boys to his hotel for dinner when he was in town. Eventually, rumors began to circulate. It was estimated that his fortune was in excess of two hundred fifty million dollars, and he had recently made it well-known that he intended to leave all of it to the Catholic Church in Central America.

When the church heard that the Father had verbalized his intent to donate his wealth, they squelched any rumors of wrongdoing on his part. In fact, a move was underfoot by the hierarchy to cement the relationship between their Father and his money. Without Nitro's knowledge, the church put a plan into place to honor him as an honorary bishop in all three countries.

When he was informed of the move to honor him, Nitro panicked. He knew the guys from Blue Seas would be able to identify him if he became any type of public figure. Additionally, he felt Bill Coade had probably built a dossier on him that would be very damning. It was too late for plastic surgery to change his face, for everyone in the church now knew him. His only option was to eliminate all the people who had known him as General TN. Once done, no amount of publicity could cause him any harm. He had anonymously put his plan of assassinations in motion, and lastly with Bill dead, he was free from any past ties. He, of course, wrongly assumed Jim Montie had died as the result of a mine explosion.

Chapter 26

The police concluded their investigation into the apparent murder of Bill Coade by evening. Jon stated that he had discovered the body himself and that no others had been involved. Jon would later arrange a small memorial service at a nearby church, and Bill's ashes would be scattered off shore into the blue waters of the Pacific Ocean. Jim and Joe stayed at the hotel and attended the memorial. They were convinced that the assassin, having completed his assignment, would move on and disappear.

They gathered the next morning for breakfast with Jon and Jerry and adjourned to the plush hotel office that had once been shared by Bill and Jon.

Jim McDonnell took the floor. "I know who is responsible for your father's death." His statement was straight to the point, for Jim was in no mood to pull any punches.

He filled Jon and Jerry in on the death of his colleagues and how years ago they, along with Bill, had operated in Laos along with the general. He explained how the general had gotten the handle Nitro and his subsequent disappearance just as the secret war had come to a screeching halt.

"Jon, by sheer coincidence, your father located Nitro just before his death at the hands of a hired gun. A gun I'm sure was hired by this Nitro himself." He held the folded newspaper for all to see.

Jon took the paper and stared at the picture of the priest with the circle around him. "So Jim, you are telling us that this priest is the former general?

"Yes, I am. I'm convinced. I'd recognize him anywhere."

Jon continued, "And you believe that he is covering up his old tracks by knocking off old friends?"

"That's it, in a nutshell."

Jon began to pace around the office as he spoke in anger. "Years ago, my father warned me about such a man. He referred to him only as General TN. He said he regretted not being able to knock him off at the end of the war." With the same breath, he continued, "Well, my friend, this isn't over yet." Jon had fire in his eyes as they met Jerry's.

Jon perused the newspaper article. "It says here that the 'Father' is going to be honored tomorrow at the town square in Managua, Nicaragua. Tell me again, Jim. Is there any doubt in your mind about this priest being the general?"

"Jon, if I had a gun and I could get close enough to this guy, I'd kill him myself."

"I'd say he was sure," Jerry broke his silence.

Jon mentally put the memorial service on a temporary hold. Joe had nothing to say. He sat there and listened, wondering where the hell this conversation was going. He didn't have to wait too much longer.

"Jerry, do you have any qualms about flying up to Nicaragua tomorrow morning in the Cessna?" Jon asked.

Jerry raised his downward cast gaze, hid a smile, and slowly shook his head left to right. "Only if you let me fly," was his only response. It was an inside joke; Jon didn't know a damn thing about flying.

"Jim, would you like to come with us and confront the priest?" Jon asked.

Jim knew that as long as Nitro was alive, his life was at risk. Possibly, he could confront his old benefactor and strike a deal with him. Although he knew that he could not trust him. He looked to Joe. "What do you think?"

"It's either you or him," Joe replied, then turned to Jon and asked, "Do you intend to kill the priest?

"Without any hesitation." Jon's reply was steely.

Joe continued after a brief pause. "Then I suggest we fly with you two up to Managua and have Jim positively identify this character as Nitro before any of us do anything as drastic as killing him."

The plan began to take shape. The Cessna left midmorning for the short flight to Managua, where Jon and Jerry were well-connected. The party of four arrived under the radar at a small dirt airstrip on the outskirts of town.

They were met there by two drivers who never spoke a word. Jerry and Jon departed in an old Toyota Camry. After an unexplained delay, Jim and Joe left in the same direction, squeezed into the front seat of a Toyota pickup truck. Their destination was the town square.

The driver dropped Jim and Joe a few blocks from the square as a crowd of about two thousand or so souls moved in unison along the arteries leading to the center square. The environment was festive, and no one seemed to notice the two out-of-place gringos moving along with them.

After the initial ceremonial introductions were completed, the sound system failed. The guest of honor, now positioned at the podium, began to speak. The crowd grew hushed and unconsciously leaned forward toward his words. Jim, with binoculars in hand, focused on the prey. Sure enough, it was Nitro in all his glory. Jim steadied the eyepiece with one hand and speed dialed Jon with the other.

"It's definitely him. No doubt about it."

Joe surveyed the crowd. There was no police presence to speak of other than two uniformed officers on either side of the gathered dignitaries some two hundred feet or so in the distance.

"All right then." Jon's reply was followed by a silent disconnect.

As the honored guest raised his arms toward the gathered mass, the first shot struck him, hitting and shattering the crystal and underlying blue face of the Rolex on his left wrist. In rapid order, the second shot blew off the top of his head. The "Father" went to his knees for the last time on this earth.

The dignitaries rushed toward their fallen hero, and the crowd began to hastily retrace their steps away from the plaza. They all knew that gunfire beget more gunfire, and no one wanted to be in the path of fire. Old fears died hard in that part of the world. Jim and Joe moved with the crowd toward their ride. They shared a brief look of concern and hoped their ride would indeed be positioned as planned. It was.

Jon was placing the scope mounted modified M14 rifle in the baggage compartment of the Cessna when Jim and Joe arrived. They had no idea who had done the actual shooting. Neither knew that Jerry was a professional killer. He had spent years as a contractor for the CIA. Bill Coade had enlisted his services several times over the years, and they had become good friends. Jerry had lived a good life at Bill's hotel, and he had just returned that favor in the only way he knew how. He was satisfied with his act of redemption, knowing full well that Bill would have approved, but he was hurting. They were airborne in minutes, flying low and slow down the coast toward the hotel airstrip. No one spoke.

Later in the day, Jon, Jim, and Joe gathered in the hotel office at Jon's request. It was late afternoon, and the drink of choice was cold beer. Jon had a shot of Jack Daniels, but the others passed.

"Joe, would you mind waiting in the lobby for a few minutes while I talk to Jim?" Jon asked.

Jim spoke up in a reassuring voice, "Jon, anything you have to say to me can be said in Joe's presence.

After Jim made his point, Jon rose from his chair behind the desk, went to the wall safe, and retrieved an envelope. He pulled up a chair in front of Jim and sat facing him.

"As I told you earlier, my father warned me about the general—Nitro, as you and Dad called him. Well, what I have here was, until recently, privilege only to Dad, myself, and a fellow named Nathan, whom I believe was your partner in BSE." He stopped and waited for a reply.

"Yes, Jon. Nathan was one of my partners who, as you now know, is deceased."

Jon moved forward a little in his chair. "The financial agreement my dad made with BSE, did it end with his death?"

"No. It survives his death and goes to any surviving family member."

"Does that include me?" Jon was extremely calm as he questioned Jim about the vast funds that flowed into the hotel from the retirement agreement between BSE and Bill Coade.

"BSE has no financial control over the funds. Your name, if I know Bill, is already listed as beneficiary. If you give me access to your computer, I can confirm this in a matter of minutes. However, if there is a glitch, BSE—which I now solely control—will personally fund a matching program for you. You certainly deserve it, and Bill would have expected me to keep you whole. Now, what does all this have to do with the envelope you have been holding in front of me since we sat down face-to-face?"

"Jim, your word is good enough for me. Here, my dad wanted you to have the information contained in this envelope. He said to me that you of all people would know what to do with it."

Jon had seen the contents only once before, years ago. The contents contained a parallel account code and password to the general's bank account in the Cayman Islands. By using this information, the entire contents of the account could be transferred out of the original account electronically and into a previously established account.

Years ago when they had all been all in Laos, the former Nathan Webster—previously known as Thatcher Pittsford—had set up all the banking accounts for General TN. At Bill's direction, Thatcher had also set up the parallel account. Bill had never trusted the general and wanted to have an ace up his sleeve. Today the ace would be placed into play.

The three of them sat in stunned silence. Joe rose, proceeded to pour three shots of Jack Daniels, and returned to his seat. They made a toast to Bill.

"Shall we get started?" Jon moved to his computer, which was located on the credenza behind the desk. The McDonnell's flanked him. Without being asked, Jon went into detail about his computer being linked to a series of servers outside the country. Thanks to Bill and his CIA background, no activity that took place on this computer could ever be traced back to the source. Once they plundered the general's numbered account, the money would be untraceable. Jon easily gained access to the account. The balance was an astounding $680,000,000.

"Give me the word, and I'll clean it out?" Jon said and waited patiently for Jim to reply.

"No, leave $3.00," Jim said.

Joe and Jon looked at him for an explanation.

Jim followed with a Bill Coade like pause before continuing.

"Tithing ... Guys, I'm tithing."

THE END

Epilogue

Early in 2002, the newly formed McDonnell Family Trust took over the day-to-day operation of the Central American Orphanages Nitro had founded with his ill-gotten fortune. The trust was extremely well-funded to the tune of six hundred million dollars. The Catholic Church of Central America no longer holds sway over the day-to-day operation of the orphanages. There is, however, an arm's length relationship established for the spiritual well-being of the orphans. Within a year, a string of sister orphanages was established by the Trust for girls.

Jim McDonnell spends six months a year in Florida at his home next door to Maggie and Joe and the balance of the year in Europe. He no longer has day-to-day responsibilities at BSE. He did, however, re-establish a relationship with an old high school sweetheart, who is now his constant companion. Maggie and Joe, along with Julia and Mike McDonnell, visit them often in Europe.

Maggie and Joe walked Julia down the aisle on the day she married Mike. Julia and Mike are co-chairmen of the McDonnell Family Trust.

The Historic McDade Mine Exhibit, located outside Scranton, Pennsylvania, which was damaged by an explosion of unknown origin, received an anonymous donation in excess of one million dollars. Repairs and improvements are underway under the watchful eye of Frank.

The university is still growing, the downtown is still changing, and Malarkey's is still prospering and is visited occasionally by the McDonnell brothers. As for the people, both past and present, who lived or are now living in the Scranton area, they are the heart and soul of the Lackawanna Valley, and the McDonnell brothers are extremely proud to be a part of that heritage.

About the Author

Joe Cawley is a native of Scranton, Pennsylvania. He relocated to the Saint Augustine, Florida, area in 2006 to pursue his love of writing. His background includes a stint at Villanova University, followed by an honorable discharge from the USMCR in 1967. He followed a sales and marketing career for years, relocating often as he accepted more challenging assignments.

Along the way, he managed to turn his childhood love of aviation into a reality by obtaining his commercial pilot's license for airplanes and helicopters. Over the years he has owned and flown a number of different aircraft and rotorcraft as a civilian pilot.

A move to Rochester, New York, brought a new beginning when he joined an upstart company in its infancy. The fledging database and software development company blossomed, and Joe bloomed with it. Eventually, becoming vice president and chief operating officer of the burgeoning company.

A bold decision after ten years brought retirement and a move, along with his wife, Margie (O'Malley), to Florida. The climate agreed with his creative bent and *Hallowed Gesture*, his first novel, was introduced in 2006. Now, four years later, *JIMBO* has come to life. *JIMBO* picks up where his previous novel left off and is the final novel in the McDonnell brothers saga.

Joe's third novel is underway and is based on a true story. *MATCHED* is a tale of a young family struggling, against heartbreaking odds, to establish their imprint on American society. Their trial of passion and grief is spread over four gut-wrenching years as they lock horns with the system, conventional society, and at times their own Department of State. Their pursuits take them halfway around the world and back, and with a little bit of luck and a lot of love, they persevere as a culturally diverse family in a Southern setting.

Credits

Various internet sources were the main resource for much of the historical information referenced in this novel. The author also interviewed individual(s) that experienced firsthand the rigors of living and existing in what was known as Indochina. He also traveled to some of the sites noted in the novel.

All reference to the CIA and Air America are totally fictional. All the characters in *JIMBO* are a figment of the author's imagination, and they are in no way related to anyone living or dead.

The villages and towns and cities are a combination of fictional and non-fictional locations. Some of the landmarks and business places mentioned throughout the novel are existing parts of the fiber and life of everyday living in those areas. For the most part, they are entities open to the public that are identified for their positive contribution to the local scene and are most worthy of a visit.

The map adorning the inside front cover is only partially accurate and is part of the fictional nature of the novel.

The Lackawanna Historical Society was extremely cooperative in providing historical information and photos. One such photo of the Gorge at Nay Aug Park is depicted on the front cover of *JIMBO*.